BUGGED!

Young Danny Partridge was just plain angry. His big brother, Keith, his sister, Laurie, his mother, Shirley, even the small-fry Christopher and Tracy —none of them would believe him when he told them about the mysterious messages he had uncovered and the grim danger that threatened their new neighbors.

All right then! He'd show them! He'd solve this mystery all by himself!

And when Danny suddenly found himself in the hands of a gang of vicious killers, it was too late for him to change his mind.

For Danny Partridge it was do or die . . .

THE PARTRIDGE FAMILY

#10:

MARKED FOR TERROR

BY VIC CRUME

CURTIS
BOOKS

NEW YORK, N.Y.

THE PARTRIDGES—

Shirley Partridge— Is "Mom" to the five talented children in the Partridge Family. Her bright, strong singing voice has helped make the Partridge Family famous from coast to coast.

Keith Partridge— Shirley's oldest son is the "man of the Family." A great help to his widowed mother, Keith plays lead guitar for the group.

Laurie Partridge— Shirley is proud of her pretty teenage daughter. Laurie's singing is an important part of the Partridge fame.

Danny Partridge— Like his older brother, Danny is great on guitar, and at eleven years old, he has a steel-trap mind for business.

Christopher Partridge—	Shirley's youngest son, is a winner on the drums. He keeps the beat for the group.
Tracy Partridge—	Baby of the Family, she gives the group plenty of singing support wherever the Partridge Family performs.

Shirley Partridge recorded a song in the Family garage with her five talented children—and the Family was destined for stardom from the first scratch of a needle! Now when they travel in a renovated old school bus painted in bright psychedelic colors, Shirley drives them—and all over the country—in search of life, liberty, and the pursuit of singing engagements.

Chapter One

BANG!

☐ It wasn't a cannonball thumping into the Partridge Family's house, but only the slam of the front door—the signal that Danny, Chris, and Tracy Partridge had begun their morning rush to the school bus stop.

From the living room window, Shirley Partridge watched her three youngest children race along the sidewalk and reach the corner only one split second ahead of the yellow bus marked *East Valley Elementary*.

"Well, the kids made it again," Shirley exclaimed to herself as she watched the three climb aboard. "Not a second too early or too late. I don't know how they do it!"

Hardly had the bus door closed on Danny's heels when Laurie, Shirley's teenage daughter, called from the top of the hall staircase. "Mom, do you think it's cold enough to wear my new coat?"

Shirley turned away from the window. "It isn't even October, Laurie," she called back, walking into the hall. "Leave it in your closet and forget it for a few weeks."

"Forget it! Mom, you don't mean forget the first sheepskin, lambs-wool, plum-color, genuine Afghan coat with—"

"With pink poppies or something all over it," her brother Keith Partridge said loudly as he came strolling out from the kitchen. He called up the stairs. "Make up your mind fast, Laurie. We're catching a ride with Barry Crandall this morning, and he isn't the world's most patient guy, you know."

"No?" Laurie called over the railing sweetly. "I hadn't noticed." But she came quickly skipping downstairs and hurried over to the hall closet.

Keith's emerald eyes twinkled as he reached for his own jacket. "I hate to tell you this," he said to his sister, "but after today we'll have our own car back. Then goodbye Barry!"

"Oh, I don't know," Laurie answered calmly. "Maybe I'll ride with you and maybe I won't. Who knows?"

"Not you!" Keith grinned. He turned to his mother. "Mom, would you call the garage for me? I forgot to tell them the left headlight burned out, and I want to pick it up after school."

"Pick up a burned-out headlight?" Laurie asked.

Keith groaned. "Honestly, Mom—I can't stand much more of Miss Partridge's witty remarks. Couldn't we send her away someplace?"

A horn sounded outside. "There's Barry now," Shirley said. "And I think I'll send you both away someplace—to school!"

In two seconds, the front door had banged shut for the second time that morning, and the two older Partridges were zooming down the steps.

Shirley watched them squeeze into Barry's small car. "Whew!" she sighed. "Mornings! When I think of those nice, calm coffee shops we go to when we're on rock tours! And how after breakfast we all pile in the same old bus and at least *go* in the same direction! Whoever said concerts and traveling are strenuous?"

"Hi, Barry," Laurie flung open the car door and

10

greeted their next-door neighbor. She slid across the seat.

"Hi!"

"Hi, Barry. Laurie, can you move over an inch?" Keith squeezed in, and Barry lost no time swinging his rather elderly car away from the curb and up the street.

"Hold it!" Keith cried out. "The door isn't closed."

Barry slowed the car as Keith tugged at the door.

"Oh, no!" Keith groaned. "Barry, the door handle's pulled loose."

"Don't give it a thought," Barry said airily. "Just roll down the window and slam it shut. After this week your neighbor will be driving a four-on-the-floor, bucket-seat new car."

"Oh, *wow!*" Laurie exclaimed.

"Yeah," Barry said cheerfully. "Dad's matching my summer savings—and I'm accepting his hard-earned dollars. Now if I were Keith Partridge, famous rock singer, these small problems would never bother me."

Keith laughed. "Better your Dad's hard-earned dollars than getting our business manager to loosen the purse strings! Man! If Reuben Kinkaid had his way, I'd still be riding my tricycle, I guess." He gave the door a slam. "Let's roll!"

"Hey, look!" Laurie exclaimed. "What's going on at the Penland place? The gates are open!"

All three looked down the long driveway on the right that led to the huge, gloomy-looking old mansion next door to the Partridge house. Several panel trucks and pickup trucks were parked near the mansion, and painters were putting up scaffolding equipment. Other workmen were tearing down boarding from the big windows, and still others were going in and out of the house, carrying things.

11

"Oh, that," Barry said, shifting gears and rolling ahead. "You're getting new neighbors. I'll bet Mom is over at your house now, telling your mother all about it. Man! She was all excited when Dad told us last night."

"About what?" Laurie asked. "Barry, you're being *maddening*."

Barry grinned. "It just doesn't hit me as being too newsworthy," he said. "But Mom remembers old Miss Anabel Penland and when the Penland mansion was the showplace of the old home town, and she knew Miss Anabel's niece. And that's why she's so interested, I guess. Anyhow, Dad's law firm handles Miss Penland's properties here, and she's been writing him all kinds of instructions. She's moving back."

There were few people in town—or maybe in the whole United States—who hadn't heard of Miss Anabel Penland. Her father's business, founded so many years ago, had grown into the giant Penland Chemical Company, and Miss Penland had become one of the nation's wealthiest women.

"Man!" Keith exclaimed. "With all the money she has, I don't think she's showing much imagination. Who'd want to live in a dismal rockpile like that?"

"Maybe she's sentimental," Laurie said. "Probably in her old age she wants to return to the scenes of her childhood. Although I must say it's hard to believe that place was ever the scene of *anybody's* childhood."

Barry stopped for a traffic light. "Well, it's about to become the scene of her orphan relatives' childhood," Barry said. "That's why she's coming back. Dad said Miss Anabel's niece, the one Mom knew, had two kids, and when the niece was killed in an automobile accident last year, the kids were orphaned because their father already had been killed—I've forgotten how, it was a long story. Anyhow, these kids have been brought up in England. And Miss Anabel's decided they should learn about America and Great-grandpa's great history, I guess."

"I feel sorry for them already," Laurie said. "But probably she'll send them away to school, so at least they won't have to be there *all* the time."

"Nope," Barry replied. "West High is to be part of their Americanization program, if you can believe it."

"This is beginning to get interesting," Keith said. "Did you happen to get around to finding out if the Penland kids are two beautiful seniors?"

Barry laughed. "Slipped my mind," he answered, turning into the school parking lot. "But their name's not Penland—it's Smith."

Chapter Two

☐ Nothing short of tearing down the old Penland mansion could change its stern, forbidding look. But Danny Partridge figured that with so many workmen on the job, even that huge, gloomy rockpile could be improved. But not even Danny could believe the change that took place in only a month's time.

Now, with shutters freshly painted and the tall, curving bay windows sparkling in the late-October sunshine, the Penland mansion looked at least livable. Maybe Miss Penland would be arriving soon.

On Saturday morning, he came rushing into the house with his latest news. "It's almost ready for people, Mom!" he exclaimed excitedly. "I know, because I've been watching the men from Elliot's Appliances. They've been moving in a refrigerator and a stove and a washing machine, and I *think* a big stereo—I couldn't quite make it out through the crating," he said excitedly.

"Danny!" Laurie exploded. "Do you mean you stood there and *snooped?*" She turned to Shirley. "Mom, really—I think that's awful. And it's gossip."

"Gossip! Me gossip?" Danny's face began to match his red hair. "I'm just giving facts! That's all! I'm not rushing around talking about how maybe the Penland kids will both be boys! And at least juniors in high school."

Laurie flushed. "I'm simply interested in people," she said stiffly.

"Well, I'm simply interested in appliances," Danny said hotly.

At this point, Shirley intervened. "Let's give the whole subject of the Penlands a vacation, kids. We're all going to be glad to meet the new neighbors, but between now and then—*whoa.*"

"Okay," Danny said angrily. "That's okay with me. *I'll* never tell any interesting facts to anyone in this house again!" He thumped out of the room.

Things might have been very different in the days ahead if Danny Partridge hadn't suddenly decided that as far as what went on at the Penland mansion was concerned, his lips were sealed!

It was the first weekend of November when the new neighbors came. They arrived after dark, and lights went on in the big old house for the first time in years. Nobody in the neighborhood saw them that night or even the next day, which was Sunday. But on Monday at school, Laurie's hoped-for new junior-class boys turned out instead to be *one* junior-class girl. And worse—a girl wearing a plum-colored Afghan coat embroidered in big pink poppies—exactly like Laurie's.

"I was never so embarrassed in my life, Mom," Laurie fumed Monday afternoon when she and Keith came home from school. "There *I* was, waiting for Barry and Keith to drive up, and suddenly there is *my* coat standing right next to me beside the curb, and there's Miss British Accent inside of it. And if that isn't enough, up swirls that big Rolls Royce—"

"That just matches the coat," Keith grinned.

"—And *she* steps in and swoops off before I can

18

even squeeze into that hideous pumpkin Barry Crandall calls a car!"

"Well, never mind, dear," Shirley said. "After all, it shows that you girls both like the same things, doesn't it? Now, not to change the subject—but you did remember to mail the light bill, didn't you?"

Before Laurie had time to look guilty, Danny Partridge came slamming into the front hall. "Hi," he greeted the family. "What do you think?" He flung his books into the nearest chair. "One of the new kids next door is in my class—and he's my *double*." Then he quickly added, "Physically only. Man! Is he dumb!"

"*He's* dumb!" Laurie exclaimed. "Danny, stop! Mother, how can you stand Danny's ego? *I* can't!" She sped out of the room.

"What's wrong with her?" Danny grinned cheerfully. "Does she want a dumb brother? Anyhow, as I was saying, honest, Mom, we do look just about alike. Even Mrs. McAllister said she thought she was seeing double—which was pretty silly, because our clothes are sure different. You should have seen how that guy was dressed! He looked like Mr. Crandall looks on his way to the office—you know, just *perfect*—tie and everything.

Keith grinned. "What's wrong with looking perfect?" he asked.

"You know what I mean," Danny replied airily. "Anyhow, Mrs. McAllister introduced him. She said, We have a new classmate—Robert Smith. Only Robert Smith didn't seem to know his own name. He just sat there and stared around as though he was waiting to see who Robert Smith was. That's why I said he was dumb."

Shirley frowned. "Maybe he's shy, or maybe he

doesn't hear well," she said. "Don't you think you're being unkind, Danny?"

"Nope," Danny answered firmly. "There's nothing wrong with his ears. I know, because after school that big car of Miss Penland's rolls up and when this kid starts to get in, one of the guys says, 'Bet he couldn't find his way home by himself.' And what happens? This Robert Smith kid turns around and *pow!*—socks him flat. Then he jumps into his car, and off he goes with his nose in the air."

"That doesn't sound so dumb to me," Keith laughed. "Always jump into your car before the other guy gets up and slugs you back."

"Keith Partridge! I heard that!" Laurie swept back into the room. "How can you say you're against violence and then *laugh* about fisticuffs in the schoolyard?"

"Fisty-whats?" Keith asked. "Will you please repeat that, madam?"

A telephone ring ended further discussion as Keith, Danny, and Laurie all rushed for the hallway, saying, "That's probably for me."

It turned out to be a call for Keith.

"Now the phone will be tied up for five hours, I suppose," Danny said disgustedly. "I might as well go upstairs."

When Laurie returned from her race to the phone, she was putting on her beloved Afghan coat. "Mom, I was going to mail your letter, and then I forgot," she said. "But I'll rush it down to the corner mailbox right now."

She reached in her pocket and pulled out a white envelope.

"That isn't the light bill, Laurie," Shirley said. "Their return envelopes are green."

20

Laurie glanced down, and a startled look came over her face. "Mom, *look!*"

The letter bore no stamp, and it had no address. But across the front, in neat capital letters, was typed, FOR PAMELA SMITH—IF THAT'S WHAT YOU'RE CALLING YOURSELF NOW.

"Somebody must have put it in my pocket when we were both standing by the curb," Laurie gasped.

"And thoughtfully taken our light bill to mail, I suppose?" Shirley frowned. "No, you must have switched coats, Laurie."

"But that's impossible, Mom. We each have our own lockers. Somebody *put* this in my coat."

Laurie was back from her call almost right away.

"What's the plan?" Shirley asked. "Is she coming here, or are you taking her coat over there?"

Laurie shook her head. "It was the oddest conversation. She sort of *whispered*. And she asked me to please keep the coat and we'd trade back tomorrow at school. And I started to say there was a letter in her pocket, and she said, 'Sorry. I have to hang up now.' And I never did get in a word about our light bill."

Shirley sighed. "I don't imagine the power company will turn off the lights. Just remember to ask about the envelope tomorrow, Laurie. *Please.*"

But later, when Shirley Partridge was alone in the living room, she thought about the new next-door neighbors. About Robert Smith—a boy who didn't seem to know his own name, and about a girl named Pamela Smith—*if that's what you're calling yourself!*

A sudden unpleasant thought struck Shirley. Betty Crandall had said Miss Penland hadn't seen those children since the boy was a baby. Maybe Miss Penland had two strangers—impostors—in her house! After all, she was one of the ten richest women in America, and the great-niece and great-nephew were her sole heirs—if Pamela and Robert Smith really *were* her relatives.

"I just think I'll call next door tomorrow," Shirley thought. "I'll invite them for dinner Saturday. I think I'd better meet those children myself. If there's anything the Partridge family doesn't need, it's one more strange adventure. And that family sounds *strange!*"

Chapter Three

☐ Laurie and Pamela met on the school steps the next morning and walked to their lockers together.

Pam held out the green envelope Laurie had forgotten to mail. "I'm sorry," she said. "I'd have posted it for you, but there actually was no—no opportunity." Her cheeks flushed pink.

Laurie's face was just as pink as Pam's. She pulled the white envelope from the coat pocket. "I found this," she said miserably. "I'm sorry, Pam. I did read the outside, but I want you to know I consider it confidential. I mean, I won't rush around talking about—" She broke off as she saw the color in Pam's face drain away, leaving it a dead white.

"Someone must have put it in your pocket when we were signing up for ski club," Laurie said in a low voice. "I mean—that's when our coats were lying on the chairs."

Pam managed a laugh. "Oh, I don't think so, Laurie. My young brother has a new typewriter, and I imagine he was just playing pranks. If you had a brother around eleven years old, you'd know what I mean."

"Oh, I have one," Laurie replied. "I know *just* what you mean. And speaking of brothers reminds me—I didn't have time to tell you over the phone, but we're neighbors. I live right next door to the Penland place, and we want you to come over. Maybe you'd have dinner with us some night soon?"

"I'd love to," Pam replied. Then she frowned. "Laurie, how far is it from here to the East Valley Elementary School?"

"East Valley?" The sudden change of topic startled Laurie. "Oh, it's miles," she answered. "Your brother is in my brother's grade, and Danny has to take the school bus, it's so far. Why? You're not thinking of rushing over there now and bopping him, are you?" She giggled.

Laurie could have sworn Pam Smith suddenly shivered. Yet Pam's voice wasn't shivery. It even had a little laughter in it. "Oh, never!" she exclaimed. "Far from that! It's just that we've been together all summer and I'm used to keeping an eye on him. And now everything is so new here."

Laurie laughed. "If I'd been with my brother Danny all summer, I'd be right out of my mind! Oh, there's the bell. We'd better run."

But as the two girls parted, Laurie looked back at Pam's disappearing figure. She had two feelings about Pamela Smith. One—that they were going to be friends. And two—that Pam hadn't quite told the truth about her brother "playing a prank." "Why did she turn white?" Laurie asked herself. "If I thought Danny had done a thing like that, *my* face would turn *red*—from absolute *rage*."

Shortly after three o'clock, Shirley Partridge rang the old-fashioned turn-doorbell of the Penland mansion. It was opened by an unsmiling maid in uniform.

"I am Miss Penland's neighbor," Shirley introduced herself. "Will you ask Miss Penland if Mrs. Partridge may see her?"

The maid shook her head. "Not home," she said.

"When is she expected?" Shirley asked.

"Not today," came the reply. And the maid began to close the door.

"Then I'll see whoever is in charge, please," Shirley said.

A voice came from the shadowy hall. "Who is it, Karya?"

The maid scowled and did not reply, but she opened the door a bit wider. Walking toward the entrance was a short, plump, rather oldish woman, dressed in black silk.

Again Shirley said, "I am Shirley Partridge, Miss Penland's next-door neighbor. Perhaps you can tell me when it will be convenient to call on Miss Penland?"

The plump woman shook her head. "Goodness knows when that will be. Come in, Mrs. Partridge. I'm taking Miss Penland's place for the time being— I'm her right hand, you might say. Gruff is the name —Mrs. Gruff."

She turned to the maid. "Mrs. Partridge and I will have a nice cup of tea, Karya, while I tell her about poor Miss Penland."

The maid shot a glance of dislike at both Mrs. Gruff and Shirley. But she went thumping off into the dimness of the big hall.

"Is Miss Penland out of town?" Shirley asked, following plump Mrs. Gruff into a large room off the hall.

"Mercy, yes!" Mrs. Gruff exclaimed. "In fact, the poor soul never *reached* town. She's in a hospital in New York."

Shirley looked at Mrs. Gruff in surprise. "In the *hospital!* Mr. Crandall never mentioned that."

Mrs. Gruff frowned. "Mr. Crandall? Who is—oh,

27

yes! The lawyer, you mean. Well, I must call him. That's a detail I have completely overlooked. He lives here, I believe?"

"Just down the street," Shirley replied.

"There's been so much to do. Poor Miss Penland! It was all too much for her. She just collapsed, and everything fell on my shoulders. All the arrangements, you know. I myself met the children at the airport, and then we came straight here," Mrs. Gruff sighed.

The maid, Karya, came in with a tray. "Set it here," Mrs. Gruff said. She glanced at the tray. "And bring tea cakes," she added.

Shirley squeezed lemon into her tea. "I'd planned to ask Miss Penland if the Smith children could have dinner with us Saturday evening. Perhaps you will give your permission?"

"Indeed! Indeed!" came Mrs. Gruff's reply. "I'm sure they'll be pleased. They don't know any young people, and they are lonesome, I'm sure. Those poor dear children don't have a soul on earth but Miss Penland. She is their only relative, and—"

There was a sudden crash in the hall. The maid came to the doorway. "I'm sorry, ma'am. The tea tray it was. The cakes—they are on the floor."

Mrs. Gruff waved her hand. "Then bring another plate, Karya."

The maid disappeared, and Mrs. Gruff sighed again. "I can't think where Miss Penland found this staff. Not a one that can speak English properly, and not a one that doesn't speak some strange gibberish in what you might call their 'private moments.' Oh, well, so much else has gone wrong that I'm glad enough to have them."

Shirley nodded. "You're very lucky. You'd have a hard time finding help in this town. Well I must run. It's nearly time for the children to be home from

28

school, and I like to be there when they arrive. Shall we say six-thirty Saturday, then? We'll call for Pamela and Robert and see them back to their own door.

Mrs. Gruff nodded. "That will be very nice. By the way, Mrs. Partridge. I notice that a school bus stops on the corner. Would you recommend it for Robert?"

Shirley laughed. "My three travel on it—if that's a recommendation."

Mrs. Gruff didn't laugh back. "There's safety in numbers, don't you think?" she asked unsmilingly.

Shirley stared. A quick chill ran along her spine. What a strange thing for Mrs. Gruff to say! Then she smiled. "Oh, you mean if all the neighborhood children ride on it, the bus must be safe. Oh, yes, Mrs. Gruff. Perfectly safe!"

Chapter Four

☐ Saturday evening, while Keith was steering the guests from next door through the gap in the bare lilac hedge, Barry Crandall was taking the shortcut from his side of the Partridge yard.

In the house, Shirley, Laurie, Chris, and Tracy were glowing with hospitality and waiting for the front door to open.

Only Danny was not in sight. "From everything I've noticed this week," he had announcd, "I don't think that Robert Smith will even show up. He's a loner. I'm going to adopt a wait-and-see attitude."

Shirley had smiled at her red-haired independent thinker. "Okay, Danny," she'd said. "But while you're waiting and seeing, take a shower. Put on your pale-green shirt, and be downstairs at 6:25 sharp. Yes?"

Danny grinned. "Yes. And Mom, if he *does* come, I bet you're going to get a big surprise!"

When Robert Smith walked into the Partridge living room, he was not just a big surprise. He was a big sensation! And not because he went straight to Shirley, held out his hand, bowed, and said, "It is a great pleasure to be in your home, Mrs. Partridge."

For a moment, Shirley was speechless. It was like seeing her own Danny Partridge standing before her —a strange, unsmiling Danny, standing stiff and straight as a board, and without one red hair out of place. But he certainly didn't *talk* like Danny.

Before she could reply, Tracy Partridge gasped, "*Oh!* It's like Danny was in the Foreign Film Festival pictures on Saturday!"

Shirley laughed. She pressed Robert's hand. "That's Tracy's way of saying we all think we're seeing two of Danny, and one of him has an English accent. Does Mrs. McAllister ever mix you two up at school?"

Not a smile touched Robert's face. "Never," he answered coolly. "I believe it is my attire that saves the day." He turned to Pam and drew her forward. "My sister Pamela—Mrs. Partridge."

Danny, who had arrived in the doorway, stood spellbound. "Man!" he thought to himself. "I can just see Laurie trailing around behind *me*. She'd be dragging me with her, and saying 'And this is my little brother Danny.' That guy Robert is *really* in control!"

By the time the guests were eating Shirley's crusty fresh apple pie, the evening was off to a big success. Everybody was talking with everybody. Even Robert seemed to be relaxing a little in the warmth and good feeling around the Partridge family table.

When they were once again in the living room after dinner, Barry said, "Why don't you get out your guitar, Keith?"

"Oh, you play that instrument?" Pamela said with interest. "I love it!"

For just a second, the famous rock star stared. It was the first time in a long while that he had met someone who didn't know the name of Keith Partridge—Keith Partridge, who played lead guitar in one of the most successful rock groups in the country. Then Keith grinned.

34

"Do you like rock music, Pam?"

Pam nodded. "Oh, yes! Actually, I collect—" She stopped suddenly. "*Partridge*. You don't mean—why, *Keith Partridge!*" She looked around the room. "You're the Partridge *Family!*" she exclaimed. "Why, I had your recordings in England! Oh, please play—do!"

"You won't have to coax him," Danny said. "Come on, Robert. Let's go upstairs. I want to show you my new tape recorder. We can try it out."

Robert hesitated.

"Come on," Danny urged. "You can hear Keith all over the house. You won't be missing a *thing*."

Two hours later, Pam glanced at her watch. She jumped up. "I feel like Cinderella," she laughed, "but Robert and I must leave. Mrs. Gruff is very strict about his hours."

At 10:25 sharp, goodnights were exchanged. The two Smiths thanked Shirley for a "smashing" time, then with Keith, Laurie, and Barry to guide them, started back the long way around by sidewalk to the Penland mansion.

In the chilly, moonlit night, the old house looked even bigger and more forbidding than in the daytime. Pam, walking close to Keith, shivered.

"It's hard for me to imagine my mother as a little girl in that house," she said. "In fact, it's hard to imagine any small children having lived there."

"Pretty gloomy," Keith agreed.

"Yet Mother used to tell me about good times there —birthday parties and things like that. So I guess it must have been quite different then."

"Didn't she ever come back for a visit?" Keith asked.

Pam shook her head. "No. Grandfather and Grandmother Penland died, and the only member of the family left was Great-aunt Anabel. And she had gone to live abroad."

"Too bad your great-aunt had to get sick just when she planned to sort of start a new life in the old home town, wasn't it?" Keith asked.

For a moment Pam didn't reply. And when she did, her voice was tense and very low. "Keith, could I trust you about something dreadfully important? I mean, trust you to keep it secret?"

"Sure," Keith replied. "But you'd better hurry up. They're all waiting for us at your driveway."

"Oh, I didn't mean *now*," Pam said. "Could we meet in the school cafeteria on Monday?"

"You sure are making this mysterious," Keith laughed. He felt Pam's arm stiffen and begin to pull away. "Aw, come on, Pam." He caught her arm. "How about my picking you up tomorrow afternoon? We could drive someplace, and you can tell me what's on your mind."

Pam shook her head. "I wouldn't be allowed to do that."

Keith stopped walking. "What do you mean you 'wouldn't be allowed'? Man! You're sixteen years old. You're not a baby."

In the moonlight, Pam's face looked pale and unhappy. "Please, Keith. I'll explain everything, but not here—*not anywhere near this house*."

Keith stared. Pam did look frightened. "Okay, then," he said slowly. "It's the school cafeteria if you say so."

Robert called back to them. "Pam, will you hurry, please? It's quite chilly, you know."

Quickly they caught up with the others, and before another three minutes had passed, the heavy doors of the old mansion had closed behind Pamela and Robert Smith.

36

Shirley was in the hallway when Keith and Laurie returned, frowning at the envelope she held in her hand.

"What's wrong, Mom?" Keith asked quickly.

Shirley looked up. "Did you see anybody on the street when you went out?" she asked.

They both shook their heads.

"I can't understand it then," Shirley replied. "Look," she held out the envelope. "This was just inside the door. *Somebody* put it there."

"What is it, Mom?" Keith asked. He and Laurie followed as their mother walked into the living room.

"Laurie and I weren't going to mention it, Keith—but when the girls switched coats the other day, there was a very unpleasant envelope in Pam's pocket. Laurie said Pam thought maybe Robert had put it there for a joke. Now look at this." She handed the envelope to Keith.

Like the first one, there was a neatly typed line across the front: FRIENDLY WARNING. Keith ripped open the envelope and pulled out the folded sheet. He read aloud: PAMELA SMITH IS A LIAR AND A TROUBLEMAKER. DON'T LET HER MAKE TROUBLE FOR YOU.

Laurie hesitated. "Mom, you don't suppose Robert *could* have left it? I mean—I guess nobody would have noticed if he'd just suddenly bent down and slipped it under the door while we were walking ahead down the front steps."

"I don't think so," Shirley replied. "He seems to be a nice boy, and more than that, he seems to be very fond of his sister. He almost acts as though *he* is looking after *her*. Didn't you think so? Besides, you said you didn't quite believe Pam when she said it was a prank."

"Some prank!" Keith exclaimed. "Looks to me as

37

though somebody doesn't want Pam to have any friends. Why tell us—even if she is a liar?"

"Keith!" Laurie exploded. "What a mean thing to say!"

Keith yawned. "Well, excuse me. I'm not going to sit around all night talking about—about nothing. Maybe Robert is a fiend. How do I know. Maybe he hates his sister. Maybe she hates him." He suddenly grinned. "*Maybe evil forces are at work in the ancient House of Penland.* Who knows? Well, I'm turning in. Goodnight, ladies!"

But as Keith walked up the stairs, he wondered about Pam. She *was* sort of dramatic—all that stuff about not talking anywhere near the Penland place and not being allowed out. She'd been "allowed out" tonight, hadn't she? "I'll bet she just has something else to do," he thought. "Monday I'll ask her to go to a movie next Saturday night. I bet she'll be 'allowed out' if she wants to be."

Then a sudden picture came into his mind—Pam's pale face in the chilly moonlight. She *had* looked unhappy, and frightened. What if something not so funny *was* going on in that big, forbidding house next door?

Chapter Five

☐ Whatever Pamela Smith was going to tell Keith at school, he wasn't going to find out on Monday. Pam didn't even come to classes.

Then when Danny came home in the afternoon, he said that Robert had been absent from Mrs. McAllister's class. "I think I'll call him," he said. "We're starting on a new science experiment." Then, his eyes twinkling, he added, "And it's absolutely *smashing*."

"Oh?" Keith raised his eyebrows. "What are you smashing? Atoms?"

"That would be *splitting*, I believe," Danny replied coolly. "Excuse me. I'll grab the phone before my many relatives get their mitts on it."

Too late. The telephone rang, and Shirley, coming into the hallway from the kitchen, answered.

Danny groaned, then pricked up his ears as he heard his mother say, "Oh, hello, Mrs. Gruff."

But after that, the conversation didn't seem to be too interesting, and Danny went back into the living room.

Shortly after, Shirley returned. "If that isn't too bad," she said. "Pam has a bad wrist-sprain. It seems she tripped coming down the stairs this morning, and her whole weight fell on her left hand. Mrs. Gruff asked if Laurie would mind picking up any assignments from school tomorrow and bringing them

41

over." Then she added, "But I don't imagine it will interfere with Saturday night."

Keith stared at his mother. "How did you know about Saturday night?" he blurted. "I haven't even asked her yet."

Shirley stared back. Then she giggled. "This conversation has a hole in it somewhere. I'll begin again. Betty Crandall is having a dinner party. Pam and Robert and all six Partridges are invited."

"Aw, *Mom!*" Keith exclaimed. "Another kid party. That makes two Saturday nights in a row."

"Well, dear, perhaps you and Barry can stand the company of kids like your mother and his parents during dinner. After dinner, we'll play bridge, and you teenagers can do whatever you please. Mrs. Gruff has promised to come to our house, and the children will be coming back here." She turned to Danny. "You and Robert could think of ten things, at least, you could do here that you couldn't do at Crandall's, and you know how sleepy Tracy and Chris get. They won't be in your way."

Danny didn't seem much interested in plans as far away as Saturday night.

"What'd Mrs. Gruff say was wrong with Robert?" he asked. "He wasn't in school either."

Shirley looked surprised. "Why, nothing. She didn't mention him." She glanced at her watch. "Goodness! I'd better get that roast in the oven." She left the room.

Danny picked up the jacket he had flung down on a chair and said, too casually, "Well, nothing's doing around here. Think I'll go out."

Keith didn't look up. "Okay," he said, absentmindedly.

42

Danny didn't take the shortcut. It was right in view of the kitchen window, and he had the feeling his mother wouldn't approve his plan, which was to personally investigate Robert's absence from school.

He hurried along the front sidewalk, then lost no time in turning up the Penland driveway and reaching the front door. He gave the turn-ring doorbell several brisk twirls and waited a moment. As nobody opened the door, he grasped the turner for another ring, and just as he did so, the big door swung inward. Danny pitched headlong into the house.

He looked up into the astonished face of a woman in uniform. She burst into a flood of whispered words —and in a language Danny had never heard in his life. Then before he could say a thing, she grabbed his shoulder, rushed him into a big, shadowy hallway, and steered him straight toward a broad, curving staircase.

Then in common, everyday English, a voice behind him said, "What is it, Karya?"

Danny turned and saw a short, plump woman come into the hall. She was staring at him in amazement. "*Robert!*" she gasped. "Where have you been? And WHERE did you get those awful *clothes*?"

Danny's first feelings of astonishment and half-fear suddenly changed to a red-hot boiling anger. "My mother gave me these clothes," he answered angrily. "And I'm not Robert. I'm Danny Partridge, and I came to see him!"

Robert's voice called from the top of the staircase. "Hello, Danny! Come on up."

"Oh my goodness!" Mrs. Gruff exclaimed. "So you're one of the Partridge children. *Well!* Robert didn't tell me he had a *double*." She beamed at Danny. "You run right upstairs. I'll send you boys some nice hot chocolate."

Danny lost no time. He fled up the stairs while Mrs.

Gruff and the maid she'd called "Karya" left the hall.

"Don't mind Mrs. Gruff," Robert said as Danny reached the second floor. "She's not exactly an expert on what-to-wear, you know." Then he lowered his voice. "Man! Am I glad you came! Follow me."

Danny followed Robert—into a big, old-fashioned bedroom where a coal fire burned in the grate of the high, tiled fireplace.

Almost the minute Robert shut the door, he turned to Danny. "Are you my friend?" he asked.

Danny blinked. "Sure," he replied. "I came over to tell you about our new science experiment. Are you sick or something?"

Robert shook his head. "I just *told* Mrs. Gruff I was. Wait a minute." He ran across the room to a big, old-fashioned brass bed and slid his hand under the mattress. He pulled out something and held it behind his back.

"What's up?" Danny asked.

"Will you promise not to show this to *anybody* if I give it to you?"

Danny nodded.

"And will you promise to do what I ask you to?"

This time, Danny didn't nod. "I don't know, Robert. But I'll promise not to say anything in case I *don't* promise to do whatever it is you are going to ask."

Robert thought a minute. "Well, that's fair, I guess," he said slowly. He held out his hand.

Puzzled, Danny looked at a small coil of very thin wire. It could have been no more than three inches long. "What is it? I mean, what do you use it for?"

Robert's voice dropped low. "This morning, Pam took a header on the staircase."

"I heard about it," Danny replied. "Mrs. Gruff called my mother."

Robert's voice dropped even lower. "Right away, I

began to think, 'why?' I mean, Pam isn't exactly the stumbling type. So while Mrs. Gruff and everybody were racing around picking her up and everything, I looked around *fast*. And there was a long wire dangling at the side of one of the steps. I figured it must have been strung right across the stairs, and that's what tripped her. I've heard of that kind of thing, haven't you? Anyhow, I raced back up here and got scissors, then raced back and snipped just this little piece. That way, they wouldn't know I'd noticed."

Danny stared, wide-eyed. "Who's *they?*" he asked in a whisper.

Robert hesitated. "I really don't know," he replied, still keeping his voice low. "I don't fancy Mrs. Gruff, would you? Much too fat. I can't see her huffing and puffing and down on her knees in the dead of night. Can you? Besides, Mrs. Gruff is not a bad sort. Quite nice, in fact, although a bit smotherly." He shook his head.

"But who could 'they' be?" Danny asked. "It must be somebody who lives here."

Again Robert shook his head. "Oh, I should hate to suspect staff."

"Who's staff," Danny asked. "The chauffeur?"

"Staff's the people who work here. That would be Remi—he's the chauffeur. Karya—you saw her. She's the maid. Then there are the Karels. She's our cook, and Otto—he's her husband—he just potters about with the furnace and jobs hither and yon about the house."

"Gosh!" Danny exclaimed. "All those people! Miss Penland must be awfully rich. Mom says you can't get help around here for love nor money. But anyhow— what we have to think about is, who'd want to trip your sister?"

Again Robert hesitated. He cleared his throat.

"That's not exactly what we have to think about," he replied. "You see, usually I'm downstairs a good ten minutes before Pam—you know how slow girls are. But this morning I was trying to get my notebook typed up to date—the one I keep for science, you know. Anyhow, I was late."

"So?" Danny asked.

"So it's simple. You see, *they* must have expected me to be the one to go crashing," Robert replied quietly.

For a moment, there was a dead silence. Then Robert said slowly, "You see, Danny, this sort of thing has happened before."

Beneath his flannel shirt sleeves, Danny Partridge felt hairs prickle up along his arms.

There was a sharp rap at the door and Robert hurried to open it. The maid, Karya, stood there holding a tray that held a steaming pot of hot chocolate, two mugs, and a plate of cookies.

"Already I have taken Miss Pamela a cup, Master Robert," she said, smiling.

"Thank you, Karya. Set the tray over there, please." He motioned to a table.

The maid nodded and came into the room. She stared at Danny, then said in a heavy accent, "I am sorry. Mistake. Like Master Robert you look, very much." She made a little bow.

It was the first time anyone had ever bowed to Danny, and for some reason it made him feel very uncomfortable. "What if she calls me 'Master Danny?'" He blushed a deep red, then replied, "Aw, that's all right. I—didn't understand what you said downstairs. What language is it?"

Karya looked swiftly toward Robert, who answered quickly, "Karya doesn't always remember English. I guess she thought she was seeing my double, Danny. We must be something of a shock when people see us together for the first time."

As soon as the maid had closed the door, Danny's mind began to race. He watched Robert pour the chocolate into the mugs. "Robert," he said. "You'd better let me take that wire to Mr. Crandall. He'd know what to do. He's a lawyer."

Robert shook his head. "No, Danny. I just want you to put it in an envelope and keep it."

"What good will that do?" Danny demanded.

Robert's shoulders sagged. He suddenly didn't look like the in-control guy of East Valley Elementary. When he spoke, his voice almost trembled. "I—I guess I'd just like to have it on the record—you know, with a *friend*."

"But Robert," Danny pleaded. "What good's a record? You want *action*. I'll tell Mr. Crandall if you don't want to."

"Oh, no!" Robert exclaimed. "Nobody. Nobody at all. You promised, Danny."

"But why not? I don't get it," Danny said.

Robert looked down at his chocolate mug. "You see," he answered slowly. "I used to tell grownups about things like this. And so did Pam. But they said it was *lying*. We gave it up." He shook his head sadly. "Then when Aunt Anabel sent for us, we thought maybe things would be better here in America, but—" he paused. "But, I guess they know where we are. They've followed us."

Once again, Danny's arms prickled. Then he made up his mind. "Okay, Robert. I'll keep that piece of wire, and I won't tell. But I'm going to figure out *something*. We're going to catch 'them.' You wait and see!"

It wasn't until Danny was hurrying home through

the shortcut that the awful idea leaped into his head. It was so chilling that he nearly forgot to duck, going through the bare lilac hedge. He stopped dead still in his tracks.

"If I'm Robert's double—and I am—what's going to happen if *they* spot *me?*"

Right after dinner, he went to his room and sat down at the desk. A half hour later, he finished the note he was writing. He folded it, dropped it into an envelope, and tucked in the wire Robert had given him. He sealed the flap and stared at the envelope. Then he carefully printed, KEITH—FOR THE RECORD. DO NOT OPEN YET.

"Whew! That's done!" he exclaimed. "Now what'll I do with it?"

Downstairs, Laurie said, "Danny's certainly being mysterious. He wouldn't open his mouth about being at the Penland place."

Shirley laughed. "Well, he said he'd never tell any interesting facts in *this* house again. Remember?"

Chapter Six

☐ It wasn't until Thursday that Pam, her arm in a silk sling, returned to classes. Keith and Barry, coming across from the school parking lot, saw the Penland chauffeur helping her out of the car.

"That reminds me," Barry said, looking toward Pam. "Saturday night the indoor skating rink is opening. So after dinner we could take the girls skating."

"*Skating!*" Keith exclaimed. "Pam ought to be crazy about that idea. There's nothing like ice skating with your arm in a sling. What's so great about going skating?"

Barry Crandall grinned. "Because it so happens that I'm a great skater. That's why. You did your guitar thing last Saturday. Now I figure it's my turn. Besides, you can keep Pam propped up, and that shouldn't be too tough." There was no chance for Keith to reply. They had caught up with Pam on the main walk.

When noon came, Keith waited outside the cafeteria for Pam. But when she appeared, at least five girls were with her. She smiled at Keith but went straight on by. Then as Keith waited, the girls carried her tray, fixed her hamburger, opened the milk container, and so on. He could see there was going to be no chance for a private talk.

51

But Pam managed to speak to him just before French class. "Thanks for being there, Keith," she said. "I guess the cafeteria wasn't such a good idea."

"How about after school, then?" Keith asked. "We could have a soda or something."

Pam shook her head. "I'll be called for rather promptly, I'm afraid."

Keith thought a second. "Then how about sending your driver home? You can tell him you're going to ride with me."

Pam flushed. "Actually, I'd better not." She looked down at the floor. "You see, I've—I've changed my mind about what I thought I wanted to tell you. I mean, for just *now*. But thanks, anyhow."

Keith laughed. "Then we could have a soda and talk about something else."

"Really, Keith. I *can't*."

Keith Partridge felt his temper rising. "It's been a great noon hour," he said shortly. "Toodle-oo, as you say in England. I'm late." And with those words he turned on his heel and strode off.

"For two cents I'd plan to have the flu on Saturday night," he said angrily to himself. "And I would, if it weren't for Barry. But he can do all the skating with Miss Pamela Smith. I'm not going to spend the evening 'propping her up.' "

At the Crandall dinner table, Danny Partridge tried not to groan aloud. He could tell from the way Mr. Crandall was beginning that the question-and-answer period was under way. "I wonder if Perry Mason talks like that at home?" Danny thought.

Mr. Crandall put down the carving knife and fork. "And what grade are you in this year, Tracy?" he asked. Then he said, "My! You are getting to be a big girl."

Next he turned to Robert. "How is school going, Robert? What's your favorite subject?"

"Science, sir," Robert replied.

Danny spoke up to help hurry along Robert's turn in being questioned. "And he gets great grades on his reports, Mr. Crandall. I think it's because he's such a great typist. Mrs. McAllister can read typing better than anything."

Shirley and Laurie exchanged a quick look. So Robert did type well!

Luckily for Mr. Crandall, who was finally running out of questions, the telephone rang just as dessert was being served. He looked almost pleased when Barry said, "It's a long distance call for you, Dad."

"Never fails," Mr. Crandall said cheerfully as he rose from his chair. "That telephone always knows when we're having dinner."

He was not gone long, and when he returned to the table he was smiling. "Now who do you suppose that was?" he asked. "Miss Penland's doctor, and he tells me that Miss Penland is making such good progress, they're afraid they can't keep her in the hospital. She'll be coming home Monday." He beamed at Pam and Robert.

For a moment Pam's face was blank. Then a look of such happiness came into her eyes that Shirley, watching her, knew instantly that Pamela Smith was no impostor.

Pam beamed back at Mr. Crandall. "That's *wonderful!* We'll take very good care of her!"

"Yes," Robert added. "She's so *old.*"

"She's not so very old, Robert," Mr. Crandall said. "I believe she wasn't very much older than your mother. Maybe ten years or so."

"That seems quite a difference," Pam said. She

turned to Mrs. Crandall. "Did you and my mother grow up together, Mrs. Crandall?"

Mrs. Crandall shook her head. "No, dear. Oh, we played together as very young children. But then your mother went off to boarding school, and somehow we always missed each other on vacations. Then, after your grandparents died—"

"Mother went to Europe—*forever*," Robert interrupted. "Pam, you know all that."

"Wouldn't Mr. Smith ever let her come back for a visit, Robert?" Tracy asked.

Robert stared at the little girl. "Mr. Smith? Who's Mr. Smith?" he asked in a puzzled voice.

There was a shocked silence around the table. Tracy Partridge was first to break it. "Who's Mr. Smith!" she gasped. "Why, Robert! How could you forget about your daddy? We've never forgotten *ours* even though we haven't had him for almost always."

If the little girl had suddenly struck him across the face, the effect on Robert Smith couldn't have been more amazing. Color seemed to drain from his face, then rise in a flood of deepest pink until it reached the roots of his red hair. And for once he seemed to have lost his usual cool manner.

It was Pam who rescued the guests from embarrassment. She burst into a fit of giggles, so wild that they sounded false. "Robert!" she exclaimed, rocking back and forth. Then she turned to the others. "Excuse me," she gasped, "but it's so *ridiculous!*" She suddenly stopped giggling and looked again at Robert, "There's actually no disgrace in having memory lapses. It's happened to lots of people who've had a *bump on the head*."

Mr. Crandall, for some reason, looked relieved about Pam's explanation of why Robert didn't seem to remember his father. "Why, of course Pam is right," he said. "Actually, I felt all along that Miss Penland shouldn't have asked us to keep Robert's memory a secret. But she wouldn't take my advice. I'm only her lawyer!" He laughed heartily at these words. "I guess she was afraid, Robert, that people might think you were—er—not quite all *there*."

"That's American for 'crackers,'" Pam said, smiling at her brother. "Don't mind, Robert."

But Robert didn't smile back. He shook his head. "I think Aunt Anabel was right. I'd much appreciate it, Danny, if you wouldn't mention this at school."

"He *never* would!" Tracy exclaimed. The little girl rushed around the table to Robert's side. "Never mind, Robert," she said. "It was mean what I said. And nobody will ever tell anybody you *ever* forgot Mr. Smith."

It was quite a moment. Shirley's eyes were misty. Laurie was almost in tears. Barry and Keith were looking embarrassed. But on Danny Partridge's face was a very thoughtful look as he nodded agreement to Robert's request.

Everyone was glad when Mr. Crandall said, "I thought we were going to play bridge, Betty."

Mrs. Crandall laughed. "Well, for goodness' sake, Arthur—let's do."

She arose, and everybody followed her out of the dining room to go their separate ways.

Chapter Seven

☐ Barry Crandall backed the family car out of the driveway. "We don't have to go to the skating rink, Pam," he said for the second time since the teenagers had stepped into the car. "Are you sure you want to?"

"Barry—why don't you just amaze us all by driving to a movie or something?" Keith said from the back seat.

Pam giggled. "Barry, believe me—if we don't go skating, I shall promptly have a fit. After getting my skates past Mrs. Gruff's watchful gaze—not to mention her disapproval of my clothes for a dinner party—I simply *must* skate up a storm!"

"Skate up a *storm!*" Laurie exclaimed, turning toward the back seat passengers. "It's a good thing Barry's mother didn't hear you say that! She almost vetoed the skating idea until Barry promised he'd keep you off your wrist and on your feet."

"Oh, I'll stay on my feet," Pam said gaily. "Actually, the sling is mostly in honor of Mrs. Gruff. I plan to wear it as a scarf tonight. All I'll need is help in lacing my skate."

And that was all the help Pam did need. Keith, far from keeping Pam "propped up," wasn't even skating. He and Laurie sat on a bench by the rink railing and watched her as she swooped and swirled across the ice with Barry.

Pam's long, fair hair was streaming back, her blue scarf and short blue skating-skirt flying as she perfectly matched Barry's expert glides and turns.

Laurie sighed. "I'm outclassed. I think we should have gone to a movie."

"She sure can skate," Keith replied admiringly.

Laurie lifted her hand to wave at the skaters as they came flashing by again. "I've never seen her look so happy though, have you?"

Keith shook his head. "Never have—and it's funny, too. I mean, hearing that her great-aunt was coming back seemed to start it. I don't mean that wasn't good news, but—"

"I know," Laurie replied. "But not all that exciting. We've never been without a family, though. Maybe we'd be just as thrilled as Pam if even one old lady showed up. I guess she and Robert haven't had such a great life, being orphans." She turned and looked at her brother. "Keith, do you believe all that about the bump on the head Robert was supposed to have had?"

"Why not?" Keith asked.

Laurie shrugged. "Oh, I don't know exactly—but there's something funny about a lot of things about them. I mean things like Pam getting those typed notes, and Robert typing so well. Then that business about Mr. Smith, tonight. And that handkerchief—" she broke off.

"What handkerchief?" Keith asked.

Laurie hesitated. "That day I wore her coat—remember?—there was a handkerchief in the pocket with the initials P.R. instead of P.S. At first I thought maybe she was secretly married."

"*Married!*" Keith hooted. "Leave it to you, Laurie! I don't suppose you even happened to think that R might be her middle initial, or that the laundry mixed things up. Man! Are you romantic!"

60

"It so happens, Mr. Un-romantic," Laurie fired back, "that when I like someone I *think* about them. And I like Pam."

"And when I like someone, I *trust* them," Keith said, sharply.

"Hi!"

The Partridges looked up to see Barry and Pam come to a gliding stop at the rink rail. "Come on, Laurie," Barry laughed. "I'm here to rescue you from your wicked brother. What have you been saying to my girl, Keith? She looks pretty mad."

"He's just being Keith," Laurie laughed, her mood changing swiftly.

"And Laurie's being Laurie," Keith grinned. "How about a cup of hot chocolate, Pam? I'm all worn out from watching."

"Love it."

"We'll meet you over at the snack bar, then," Barry said. "Come on, Laurie. Let's swing around a few times. Okay?"

Pam floated a marshmallow in the chocolate mug and began stirring it. "You know, Keith, it's been such a wonderful time tonight." She looked up at him. "And best of all is just being thankful I didn't talk with you at school."

"You say such nice things," Keith laughed. "It was your idea, you know. But if you're thankful, so am I."

Pam flushed. "I guess I owe you an explanation," she said. "Last week I was *scared*. You see, I'd developed a pretty wild idea—I thought maybe Great-aunt Anabel was—" she hesitated "—dead."

Keith stared, and Pam hurried on. "I told you it was wild. But anyhow, now that her doctor has called Mr. Crandall, I realize just how batty my theory was."

"I don't get it," Keith said. "What gave you such an idea, anyhow?"

Pam stirred her chocolate again. "Robert and I have had rather an odd sort of life, you see. I won't bore you with all that. But so many strange things seemed to happen to us before we left England. And then they kept right on happening after we came here. Right away, Aunt Anabel isn't there to meet us. Then we hear she's in a hospital. Then they don't even take us to see her. We're whisked away to that big, gloomy old house and—and everybody seemed to be *spying* on us."

"How do you mean?" Keith asked.

"Well, Mrs. Gruff—she's a darling, but she's a kind of jailer, too. The only time Robert or I are ever alone is when we go to our rooms. As long as we're with people—I mean in school, or a party, or something, Mrs. Gruff doesn't seem to mind. But my goodness! We're hardly allowed down the front steps *alone*.

"Anyhow, I began thinking—what if something had happened to Aunt Anabel? We'd be awfully rich, I suspect. And what if somebody wanted all that money we will inherit? They'd get rid of Aunt Anabel, wouldn't they? And then—well, after Aunt Anabel was gone, Robert and I would be next on the list, wouldn't we?"

"Pam, you remind me of my sister," Keith sighed. "In fact, your imagination is *better* than hers. You're right about one thing—your theory really is 'batty.' You said it yourself."

Pam laughed. "You're probably right. But anyhow, what I've told you about feeling rather *jailed* is true. And those typed notes haven't helped either."

"But you told Laurie that Robert typed those letters," Keith said.

Pam shook her head. "Oh, no. I just thought it was better to say that to make it seem—unimportant. You know—just a prank."

"Then who sends them?" Keith asked—and was instantly sorry he'd asked.

The happy look that Pam had been wearing all evening left her face. "I *am* silly," she said. "Who does? Nothing's really changed at all by that telephone call to Mr. Crandall. Maybe the Aunt Anabel who's coming won't be the *real* Aunt Anabel at all. And if I try to tell anyone, who'll believe me? You don't, do you? *Pamela Smith is a liar*," she said, hopelessly.

She looked across at Keith and saw that he was staring past her shoulder.

"Maybe I do believe you," Keith said in a very low voice.

Pam stared.

"Look up in that mirror over the snack bar," Keith said. "See that man in the black leather coat? He's walking away."

Pam looked. Her face began to pale.

"It's that Remi—your chauffer, isn't it?"

She nodded. "Where was he?"

"Right in back of you. I just happened to look past you, and I saw his ear." Keith hesitated. "I think it must have been listening so hard that my *eyes* heard it."

To his surprise, Pam giggled. "I'm glad of it," she said unsteadily. "Now maybe *one* person in this whole world won't think I make up mad stories."

"Hey—here come Barry and Laurie," Keith said.

"You won't tell them, will you," Pam quickly asked. "Let's pretend it didn't happen. It's been such *fun* until now."

"Okay, I won't tell them. But tell them what,

anyhow?" Keith shrugged. "Talk about imagination! Mine's pretty good. For a minute there, I forgot—it's a free country. Why shouldn't your chauffeur have a night out? He was probably sitting there before we came!"

But on the way home, as Pam chattered away gaily to Laurie and Barry, Keith was very quiet. "Of course those kids are watched," he thought. "Probably that Remi is really a bodyguard. He's big enough. Probably Miss Penland hired all of them to make sure Pam and Robert aren't kidnapped for ransom or something."

He decided to keep this idea to himself. There wasn't much point in telling Pam. She'd only worry about all those silly things she'd said, things that Remi probably was laughing about right this minute. Or worse—she'd begin worrying about being kidnapped.

Then just as he had convinced himself that he'd solved whatever *needed* solving, he thought of the notes again. "Robert must have sent them," Keith decided. "There's probably more wrong with that kid than memory lapses."

Chapter Eight

□ While Pam and Barry were whizzing around the skating rink, up in Danny Partridge's bedroom Danny was discussing the future with Robert.

"I have to look ahead," Danny said. "I hate to say it, but half my family is really getting on in years. The day may come when I'm their sole support—I mean, along with Chris and Tracy, of course. Anyhow, I've been working out some original stuff I could do alone in case Chris and Tracy want to break up the act."

He picked up his guitar and strummed out a melody. "How do you like it?" he asked.

Robert nodded. "Sounds very good to me. But doesn't it need some words? I mean, most rock groups do use words, don't they?"

Danny sighed. "That's my only problem—words. "Say, Robert!" His eyes lit up. "You're great with words. Why couldn't we collaborate? You could do words, and I could do music."

Robert looked thoughtful. "Why not?" he replied. "It shouldn't be difficult, should it? I mean—weren't some of the biggest hits written on tablecloths or menus or objects like that? So it couldn't have taken too long. After all, I shouldn't imagine a song writer would spend several days in somebody's restaurant writing on the tablecloths."

67

"Man! That's right," Danny exclaimed. "Why don't we get started now. I don't have a tablecloth, but you can use my desk, and—" he stopped and eyed Robert keenly.

"And what?" Robert asked.

"Robert, I just thought of it. What if I were *depending* on you sometime, and right in the middle of writing the words, you'd have one of your memory lapses? I mean, there you'd be writing away and suddenly forget why."

Robert grinned. "I wouldn't worry, Danny," he answered easily. "My main trouble seems to be with the name 'Smith.' That's about the only thing I forget."

"I've noticed that," Danny said. "Why, do you think?"

Robert shrugged. "I think I'll write a song about it. Do you have any paper?"

While Danny went over the music again, Robert sat at the desk and wrote. He finally turned around. "How's about this?" Robert asked.

> "Bump on the head
> Bump on the head
> Not so bad as being dead.
> Then you'd even forget
> Your bump on the head."

Danny looked embarrassed. "I don't know, Robert, I think you have to work over those last two lines. I mean, I'd either have to sing, 'When you will for-*gedd* your bump on the head,' or I'd have to sing, 'When you will forget your bump on the *hett*.'"

Robert nodded. "You're perfectly right. Just a minute." He turned back to the desk, and Danny began strumming his guitar again.

"How's this?" Robert asked after a few minutes.

"Not so bad as being dead.
But I may get a bump on the head
Because somebody *wants* me dead."

Danny groaned. "Robert, you've never been to a rock concert. I can see that! Can you imagine eight thousand people all rocking and thumping with me singing about how somebody wants me dead?"

Robert yawned. Then he rested his chin on the chair-back. "I guess not. Maybe I ought to give up being a songwriter. But thanks anyhow, Danny."

"That's okay," Danny answered. "What do you think you'll be instead? Have you ever thought about it?"

Robert flung himself across Danny's bed. He stared up at the ceiling. "Oh, I don't know. Maybe—" he broke off his words and sat up. "Listen, Danny, what did you do with that piece of wire I gave you?"

"Put it in an envelope like you said," Danny replied. "Why?"

"Well, I've sort of changed my mind," Robert answered. "After all, having it tucked away in an envelope—what good does that do?"

"That's what I tried to tell you," Danny replied. "I said I'd take it Mr. Crandall and tell him what happened."

"And I said he'd think I was making it up. And now, since Pam told the world I'd been hit on the head, he'd probably be *sure* I was making it up," Robert said gloomily.

Danny sighed. "Robert, listen—why don't you level with me. I'm your friend, aren't I?"

"I certainly hope so," Robert said. "What do you have on your mind?"

Danny took a deep breath. "Robert Smith," he said. "I just don't happen to think that is your name. You can say I'm wrong if you want to—but don't get mad."

For a minute Robert didn't answer. And then he said slowly, "No, you're not wrong."

"Then what *is* your real name, and why don't you use it?" Danny asked.

Robert hesitated. "Would you swear not to tell?"

Before Danny could answer, there was a sharp rap at the door, and Mrs. Gruff opened it. "Whatever are you boys chattering about?" she asked.

Robert sprang off the bed. "We're making up music, Mrs. Gruff. Would you care to hear some of it?"

Mrs. Gruff laughed. "At this hour? Mercy me! Come, Robert. The young people have arrived, and we're going home."

As the boys followed Mrs. Gruff down the stairs, Danny made up his mind that he couldn't wait until Monday to hear more about the mystery that was going on next door. It needed solving right away.

Robert must have been thinking the same thing. At the door he turned and said to Danny, "Then you'll come over tomorrow as *planned?*"

"Sure," Danny grinned. "What time was I supposed to come?"

"How about three o'clock?" Robert asked.

"See you then," Danny replied. "I'll bring my tape recorder in case you get any song ideas."

Chapter Nine

☐ Sunday noon, Laurie Partridge looked out at the bleak November scene beyond the living room window. "In my opinion," she sighed, "November is a stupid month. Nothing happens in November—*ever*."

Keith picked up the sports section of the Sunday paper. "Oh, I don't know about that. There're *some* things."

"Like what?" Laurie demanded.

Keith grinned. "Presidential elections for one."

"Oh great," Laurie said gloomily. "That's every four years."

"How about Thanksgiving, then? That's every year, and its next Thursday."

"That's what I mean about November," Laurie replied. "Here's Thanksgiving vacation coming up, and what can you do with it? Nothing—unless you play football, which I don't happen to do."

Shirley came into the room. "Keith," she asked, "would you mind going out to the garage and helping Chris with his bike? The seat is either too high or too low. I don't remember. Anyhow, he can't manage the pliers by—" She broke off as the telephone rang. "I'll get it," she said.

Keith and Laurie perked up their ears when they realized that Reuben Kinkaid, the Partridge Family business manager, was calling from New York. Usually Mr. Kinkaid's calls meant that something exciting might be in the offing—and this call was no exception.

"You don't mean it!" they heard their mother exclaim. "But what about costumes? I don't see how—Oh! December 28th. I thought you said November. But Reuben—that's wonderful. Wait until I tell the kids!"

Before the conversation was over, all five Partridges had gathered in the living room—even Chris, who must have sensed out in the garage that something important was going on in the house.

When Shirley put down the phone, her face was glowing with excitement. "What do you suppose, kids? You'll never guess!"

"Then tell us right away," Keith suggested, his eyes twinkling.

"What would you say to a California rock concert *featuring* the Partridge Family?" Shirley asked.

"When?" Chris asked eagerly.

"Right after Christmas," Shirley replied. "December 28th."

"Would we drive the bus?" Tracy asked.

"Never!" Shirley laughed. "We'll fly to Hollywood. We can have Christmas right here, and then leave probably the day after."

"Mom, what about costumes? Are we having new ones?" Laurie asked.

"Absolutely!" Shirley answered. "You boys will have red velvet pants and white satin shirts. And, Laurie, I told Mr. Kinkaid that you and Tracy and I will take a vote on pants suits or skirts. I'm to call him back."

"White satin shirts!" Keith exclaimed. "Mom, you're sure you and Mr. Kinkaid aren't overdoing this, are you?"

74

"What about music, Mom?" Danny inquired. "New stuff, or what?"

"Both," Shirley nodded. "And we'll really have to settle into some solid practice sessions. Agreed?"

"Maybe I could let you use a couple of things I've been working up," Danny said generously. "They're—"

Again there was the sharp ring of the telephone. "I'll get it," Chris said, and rushed out to answer it. "For you, Mom," he called from the hall. "It's Grandpa in Florida."

"Grandpa!" Shirley exclaimed worriedly. "Something must be wrong. You know how Grandpa hates telephoning." She flew from the room.

Once again the family listened to a one-sided conversation and, this time, knew the news wasn't good.

"What's wrong, Mother," Laurie asked as Shirley, frowning, came back into the living room.

"Nothing too terrible, dear," Shirley answered. "But bad enough. Grandma's in the hospital. It seems she was riding in a friend's car, and they were in a minor accident. No bones broken, but Grandma was pretty shaken up and bruised, so the doctors want her to stay in the hospital for two or three more days. It's really Grandpa I'm worried about. You know how he fusses, and that will bother Grandma more than the accident." She hesitated. "There's really only one thing to do—I'd just better go down there and help Grandpa organize."

"Organize what?" Tracy asked.

Shirley smiled. "Oh—find a housekeeper to look after things for them and show the housekeeper how to get things running smoothly. Otherwise, Grandma and Grandpa both will be in a state of nerves."

"How soon would you go, Mom?" Keith asked.

"Right away," Shirley replied. "That means probably tomorrow."

"Can I go too, Mom?" Chris asked. "I bet Grandpa would like to see me."

"Me, too!" Tracy squealed. "Grandpa would like to see *me*. And I bet Grandma would too."

Shirley laughed. "And miss a week of school? I don't think so, but I'll certainly give them your love."

"But school's out Wednesday noon," Chris said. "It'll be Thanksgiving vacation."

"Thanksgiving!" Shirley exclaimed. "I forgot all about it!" She turned to Laurie, a worried look on her face. "Laurie, if I took Chris and Tracy with me, do you think you could manage a turkey for you and Keith and Danny?"

All the Partridges burst out laughing. In the midst of worries about Grandma and Grandpa, and knowing that with a concert date coming up, practice time would be so important, Mom had found a new worry —a happy Thanksgiving Day for each and every member of the Partridge Family!

"There's one thing, though," Shirley said, half-laughing, "December 28th is a really important chance for us, and we just *must* be extra-good. And that means—"

"Practice," Keith laughed. "Mom, don't worry. We'll keep on top of everything, won't we, Laurie?"

"And as I *started* to say," Danny spoke up, "maybe we can work up some new material from a couple of things I've been working on."

"New material!" Shirley exclaimed. "That reminds me—we'd better make out a grocery list right away, Laurie. In fact, we've a million things to do. Keith, will you call the airlines about schedules and reservations?"

Within the next five minutes, every member of the

Partridge Family was off on some special assignment —everyone but Danny Partridge. And for the first time he could remember, Danny felt out of everything. Keith had sounded as though he and Laurie were the only ones who were important to the group. And worst of all—Mom's reaction. "New material," Danny thought angrily. "And all she said was, we need *groceries*."

At the moment, Shirley came flying into the living room. "Now where did I leave my watch? Help me look, Danny, will you?"

Without getting up from his chair, Danny reached his hand to the lamp table beside him. "Here it is," he said, holding out his mother's tiny wristwatch.

"Oh, thanks." Shirley slipped it on her wrist. "Danny, you might get down the luggage from the upstairs hall closet. We'll need—" She looked sharply at Danny and paused. "Danny, you're not really worrying about satin shirts, are you?"

He shook his head.

"Well, you don't look very cheerful." Then an odd look flitted over her face. "Danny, you don't mind not going to Grandpa's this time, do you?"

"Nope," Danny answered shortly. "In fact, if I'd been *asked*, I'd have had to say no. I have quite a few things planned around here. For instance, I'm supposed to be over at Robert's house pretty soon. So I'd better get the luggage out now."

Shirley frowned. She hadn't forgotten the strange scene at the Crandall dinner table the night before, when Robert had behaved so oddly. What if his head injury had resulted in something more serious than memory lapses. *Someone* had typed those mean notes, and maybe that someone was a boy who wasn't— well, quite *normal*.

"Nonsense! What am I thinking of?" she said to

herself. "His own sister would know if Robert's typewriter had been used. And Pam certainly had come to his rescue when he was so embarrassed about not remembering 'Mr. Smith.' Poor Robert—he needs friends."

In her sudden sympathy for the look-alike next door, she bent down and gave Danny a quick hug. "Okay, Danny. You run along. Just remember—while I'm gone, don't you bother Mrs. Gruff. She's not used to boys—I can see that—and with Miss Penland coming home, she probably feels she has lots to do."

As she hurried out of the room, Danny almost had to blink back tears. "All I'm supposed to be is not a *bother*. Maybe I won't *bother* to go to Hollywood with them." And then he added, bitterly, "They probably wouldn't even miss me around here, the way things have been going lately."

So it was in this mood, so unlike the usual Danny Partridge, that he marched upstairs, slammed luggage out of the closet, then hurried to his room to get his tape recorder—and leave.

Chapter Ten

□ When Danny, lugging the tape recorder, rang the Penland bell, it was Pamela who flung open the door.

"Hi, Danny," she said gaily. "Come on in. Robert's around here someplace." She closed the door behind them. "We've just been flying around ever since noontime."

"Why?" Danny asked.

Pamela laughed. "Great-aunt Anabel called—Robert and I both talked with her. And she'll be here tomorrow! Remi's already started for New York to drive her back. And you can imagine how excited Mrs. Gruff is. I guess being in charge here has been quite a strain for her. Anyhow, she said that she's so happy that she has to lie down and *rest*."

Danny shook his head. "Maybe that's what old people do when they're happy." He suddenly burst out laughing. "Imagine saying, 'I'm so happy I have to take a nap.'"

"Hi, Danny," Robert came hurrying down the stairs. "What's so funny down there? Say, did Pam tell you our news?"

Danny nodded. "We've got news, too. This must be the day for telephone calls."

"What's yours?"

"For one thing, Mom's taking Chris and Tracy to Florida tomorrow."

81

"Good heavens!" Mrs. Gruff suddenly appeared in the hall. "Your mother isn't leaving you children alone, surely!"

"Oh, no," Danny said, turning to Mrs. Gruff. "She's *taking* the children. And the rest of us won't be alone. They're three of us."

Mrs. Gruff seemed to be in a much merrier mood than usual. She beamed at Danny. "That's so, indeed! And how nice for your mother to have a vacation. I don't know what I'd do if I'd had *five* young people these past weeks." She smiled fondly at Pam and Robert. "I could scarcely manage two."

"Well, let's go up to my room," Robert said. "Here, let me take that recorder. You must have a broken arm by now."

"Run along," Mrs. Gruff said graciously. "I just came out of my room for a tup of kea—I'm so excited."

As she turned away, the three started up the stairs. "What's a 'tup of kea'?" Danny whispered.

"A cup of tea, I should imagine," Robert giggled, keeping his voice low.

"Oh." Danny was disappointed. "I thought it was something new."

To Danny's further disappointment, Pam followed them into Robert's room. He was pretty sure he'd hear no secrets from Robert until she left—*if* she did.

"What are you boys planning to do?" she asked, walking over to the fireplace and adding a few lumps of coal to the grate.

"Oh—no plan," Robert said. "Why?"

"I was just wondering," Pam replied. "I guess I'm like Mrs. Gruff—excited."

"Maybe you need a tup of kea," Robert suggested.

"Oh I don't think so," she replied, smiling.

"I've an idea, Robert," Danny said. "Why don't we go outdoors? You know—explore around."

"Excellent idea," Robert replied.

"Great!" Pamela added. "I'll go get my jacket and be with you in a minute."

Danny managed not to groan aloud, and Robert quickly said, "Wait a minute, Pam. I've a better idea. Let's explore the house—I mean the third floor and the turret rooms."

"You've been here all this time, and you haven't looked it over?" Danny asked, astonished.

"Good reason," Pam answered. "There's no heat up there. It must be freezing. Even with the staircase blocked off, so much cold drifts down that I don't think we'd really survive on this floor if it weren't for the fireplaces."

"Well, for exploration purposes, it won't be any colder up there than it is outdoors," Robert said. "I vote for staying inside."

Pam shook her head. "Thanks, but some other time for me—probably a hot day in July!" She walked over to the door. "Maybe I'll call Laurie and ask her to come over."

Danny hesitated. "I guess she couldn't, Pam. She's helping Mom get ready to leave tomorrow. Mom's trip is sort of sudden because our grandparents need her. And—say! I didn't tell you the really big news! We're all going to Hollywood to do a rock concert right after Christmas."

"Oh, wow!" Pam exclaimed. "Are you lucky!"

"Are you going to let your family use any of your own music, Danny?" Robert asked.

Danny flushed, suddenly remembering how nobody at home had even seemed to notice his offer. "I'm saving it," he said shortly. "Besides, the lyrics aren't ready."

83

"Well, there's your tape recorder," Robert said, pointing across the room. "Maybe I could still think up some words."

Danny burst out laughing. "I'm sorry, Robert," he gasped. "But everytime I think of that great, gloomy lyric you turned out last night, I can't stand it! *Bump on the head maybe I'll be dead.* Wow!"

Pam's hand tightened on the doorknob. "What's that all about?" she asked sharply, looking at Robert.

"Oh, nothing," he answered, and quickly turned to Danny. "Say—how about something like this? Of course I just thought it up, but I could polish it later if you like it. 'I'm going to explore the upper floor of the house next door.' What do you think?"

"Doesn't grab me," Danny grinned.

Robert sighed. "Okay—but I really can't understand why you bothered to bring the recorder if you didn't want to have me on tape."

"You're better *live*," Danny grinned.

"Better live than dead," Robert replied, almost absentmindedly.

"Robert! For goodness' sake—*stop it!*" Pam exclaimed, and to Danny's amazement, he saw her face had turned pale.

Robert shrugged. "Just a joke," he said. "Well, let's get started, Danny. I'll get a couple of sweaters for us. It really will be cold."

Danny shivered. In the darkening November afternoon the deserted third-floor rooms looked bleak and uninteresting. Half of the rooms were along a separate hallway that led to a narrow back stairs. Robert said that they probably led down to the kitchen. "I guess servants used to live up here," he said, peering down the closed staircase. "Let's go over on the other side of the house and see what's there."

The remaining rooms were as bare and cheerless as the others had been. "There aren't even closets to look in," Danny said disappointedly. "I thought we'd find at least *one* mysterious room with cobwebs and everything. Or maybe some ancient trunk stuffed with a dead body or something."

"Cheer up," Robert grinned. "We still have the two turret rooms to explore. Maybe we'll have better luck there."

The main hallway ended in a short T-shape. At the left and at the right was a single door. The boys tried the left-side door first, and went up a short, narrow flight of steps. The top step ended at the floor level of the turret room.

"Hey! Al set for company!" Danny exclaimed, as his head and shoulders emerged into the room. "Look!"

The room was round, like the turret itself, and the walls were stone with three narrow windows cut into them. Slits of gray light came through the old-fashioned wooden shutters—just enough light so that the boys could see one single piece of furniture: a narrow metal cot. It was neatly covered with a rough blanket.

"Probably somebody put that blanket there about sixty years ago," Robert said. "Ugh! Come on, let's try the other turret room. There must be *something* interesting in this place."

As they turned to go back down the stairs, Danny noticed a square bundle on the floor. He bent down to investigate. "Aw, it's just canvas," he said. "I thought maybe we'd found something."

"Maybe that explains the blanket on the cot," Robert said. "Maybe when the painters were here, they'd come up and take a nap. At least, I can't think of any other reason. Can you?" Then he burst out laughing.

"This is some great adventure! If the other room isn't more exciting than this, I'm for speeding downstairs. Come on."

If there was anything exciting in the remaining turret room, the boys were doomed not to discover it. It was exactly like the left-side turret room—one metal cot and one bundle of canvas. But lying on the floor near the cot was an envelope. Robert stooped to pick it up. "Can't read it in this light," he said. "Probably one of the workmen dropped it."

"Well, take it along," Danny urged. "Maybe it's a long-lost will. Maybe it's a map to find the family jewels or something. Anyhow, it's the one thing we've *found*."

"Okay," Robert answered. "But I'm afraid you're going to be disappointed. It doesn't feel old. It isn't even dusty." But he folded it over and stuck it in his hip pocket.

As the boys clattered down the stairs to the third floor and hurried along the icy chill of the main hallway, Danny said, "Say, Robert—you're missing your big chance to tell me."

"Tell you what?"

"You know—'the Real Life Story of Robert Smith.' Probably Pam will come back to get our report on the sights up here, and then pretty soon I have to go home."

Robert didn't answer until after they had reached the wooden door that was set into the thin partition that blocked off the big second-floor staircase. As he closed the door behind them, he said, "It's actually *tropical* down here, isn't it. Come on. We'll do our real thawing-out by the fireplace."

As they passed Pam's room, Robert knocked at her door. "Just thought you'd like to know," he said as she opened it. "Our exploring trip was a complete zero."

Pam laughed. "I can believe it. Your nose is turning blue."

"Well, see you later," Robert said. "Maybe Danny and I are going to play chess."

Once in Robert's room, Danny lost no time in saying that he didn't want to play chess.

"Neither do I," Robert replied. "But you can get an awful lot of privacy when you say maybe you're going to play chess."

Chapter Eleven

☐ Robert held out his hands to the warmth of the grate. " 'Smith,' " he began, "was Great-aunt Anabel's idea. She wrote us, saying that using that name might save us trouble at the airport in case reporters were around."

"Why didn't she want you to use your own name?" Danny asked.

"Well, our name name had been in the newspapers quite a bit," Robert replied. "Anyhow, Pam and I agreed. So we came to New York. And then Great-aunt wasn't at the airport to meet us, and Mrs. Gruff called us 'Smith,' so we thought maybe Aunt Anabel meant us to keep on using it. Then when we came here and Mr. Crandall called us 'Smith,' we decided that either Aunt Anabel told him that was our name or told him not to say who we we really were."

Danny wriggled impatiently. "Honestly, Robert—couldn't you make this faster? Who *are* you?"

Robert sighed. "Prince Rupert Otto Alexis Robert, Prince of Carpathia," he said.

Danny stared, his eyes open wide. "You mean you are some king's son?" he asked. "But I thought you were British."

"Pam and I were brought up in England," Robert replied. "But our father was the Prince of Carpathia. Now that he is not living, I'm the Prince."

"I thought princes were the sons of kings," Danny said, puzzled.

"Not in a country like Carpathia," Robert replied. "Anyhow—even in Carpathia times have changed. Titles aren't exactly popular there anymore."

Danny looked down at his shoes. "I hate to tell you this, Robert," he said, "but I've never heard of a country called 'Carpathia.' Where is it?"

"Remember Transylvania, where Count Dracula came from?" Robert asked. "Carpathia is almost next-door."

"Wow! Do you have vampires and werewolves?" Danny asked.

"I really don't know," Robert replied. "You see, I never laid eyes on Carpathia. I was born in England. You see, Danny—around about the time I was born, royalty was going out of style in Carpathia. My father really didn't mind. He was all for having a democracy. But he didn't get anywhere with the idea, so he and my mother fled to England. Then in England he kept on working for a democratic government, and it made a lot of Carpathians really mad. Anyhow some were for him, and some were against him. And the ones against him wanted to—to—*kill* him." Robert swallowed hard. And then, in a low voice, he said, "And they did."

Danny was silent for a moment. Then he said, slowly, "I guess this isn't something you could much enjoy talking about. Okay, Robert. You're Prince Rupert, and I won't mention that at school. You needn't tell me more. I guess you don't want to."

Robert shook his head. "Now I've started, I want to tell you the whole thing." He paused and then began again. "Even in far-off Carpathia they've heard of the Penland Chemical Company, I guess. Pam and I figured it out. Even though they don't want us back as a ruling family, they'd just as soon have us back as the ones who'd inherit the big shares in the Penland Chemical Company. We think that *they* think it would really put Carpathia on the map."

"I don't understand," Danny said.

"Well, if Pam and I inherit Aunt Anabel's shares, then they figure the present government of Carpathia would inherit *our* shares. They figure they'd have our shares when we're dead."

"But right now, your Aunt Anabel isn't dead," Danny said. "And you're not either."

Robert stared at his hands. "No, we're not. Not yet," he said in a low voice. "You see, that was why I was so worried when Pam tripped and fell on the stairs. I thought it wouldn't have happened if Aunt Anabel wasn't *already* dead. I thought they were *starting on us.*"

At this grim statement, Danny's skin prickled into goosebumps. He stared at Robert.

"Of course, now that we've actually talked with Great-aunt, we're not so worried," Robert went on. "But we'll still feel better when we actually *see* her."

Danny looked into the soft flames that curled around the coals in the fireplace. Then he turned to Robert. "You know—I think I have a great idea. It could solve everything."

"Oh?"

"As I understand it," Danny began, "they don't want you back in Carpathia in case you're royalty or a democrat or something? Yes?"

Robert nodded.

"And because you're a prince the way you are, all they want is the money you get when you inherit your Great-aunt Anabel's money, isn't it?"

Again Robert nodded.

Danny leaned back and smiled. "Well—then it's

simple. Just tell your Aunt Anabel you don't want her to leave you any money, and then drop a note to the Carpathian government and tell them that even if you're a prince, you're a *poor* prince. I believe they'd lose interest, Robert."

Robert shrugged. "That would be very good advice, Danny—but you don't have all the facts. You see, as long as there are any Penland relatives living, they're stuck with the shares. It's a family kind of thing. Pam and I are the only Penland heirs left, and—well, *we're* stuck with it."

Danny sighed. "I never knew being rich could be such a problem," he said. "Well, I'd still call in Mr. Crandall, if I were you. I think you need legal advice."

Robert nodded. "We plan to talk it over with Great-aunt Anabel," he said. "We think she'll have some good ideas, too. After all, she scarcely wants to be bumped off just because she's our great-aunt."

Again a silence fell between the two boys. Then Danny looked up. "Do you have any idea yet about who strung that wire across the staircase?"

Robert shook his head.

"What about Remi and Karya? What about the fellow you call 'Otto' and his wife, your cook? They sure don't sound like British people to me. Are they from Carpathia?"

Robert nodded. "But Otto and his wife worked for us in England for years. And they were the ones who hired Karya and Remi. I don't believe they're on the other side, Danny. They believed in my father and what he was trying to do."

"But it *had* to be somebody," Danny insisted. "There's only Mrs. Gruff left."

Robert seemed to shake out of the mood he was in. He laughed. "Danny, if you can imagine Mrs. Gruff as a plotter from Carpathia—well, I can't. She's been with Great-aunt for years, and about the only thing wrong with her is that she's scared to death something will happen to us. Honestly, one reason I'll be glad when Great-aunt is back is because Mrs. Gruff has just about had it. I think *she* thinks she's some kind of baby-sitter, and she almost can't stand it—and neither can we!"

Danny thumped his head back against the chair. "Well, okay. But you'd better begin thinking about who *did*—not who didn't. That's all I can say."

There was a sharp rap at the door. "Come on, boys," Pam called. "Dinner."

"Dinner!" Danny exclaimed. "Hey, what time is it? I'd better cut out for home. They'll be expecting me."

In the chilly dark, Danny took the long way home along the front sidewalk. He had an uneasy feeling he couldn't quite understand. "I guess it's all that talk about murders," he told himself, glancing back at the gloomy old mansion with its twin turrets even darker than the dark night.

Maybe the Penlands were as rich as Ft. Knox. Maybe Robert was a multimillionaire prince. But Danny Partridge knew there was only one thing in the world for him! And he already had it! He played second guitar in the most wonderful rock group in the country. And better yet, he was a member of a noisy, cheerful, love-each-other family. Whether they wanted his music or not, Danny was a member of The Partridge Family!

And suddenly he broke into a galloping run.

Chapter Twelve

☐ If Shirley Partridge could have glimpsed the events of the coming week, she would have packed up her entire family and taken them off to Florida.

Even before she and Chris and Tracy boarded the Florida-bound plane late Monday afternoon, the wheel of chance had begun its fateful circling. Luckily or unluckily, Shirley didn't know. She waved a final goodbye to her teenagers and middle son.

From behind the fencing the kids watched the big plane taxi down the field, turn, and thunder back past them. As it lifted into the sky, Danny sadly said, "I hope they're not sky-jacked with me not along."

"I'd hope that even if you *were* along," Laurie said grimly. "And that's saying a lot."

Keith reached into his jacket pocket. "Let's take a look at the note Mom gave me last thing."

In the stiff breeze blowing across the field, Keith opened the envelope. "Hey! Money! Good thing I looked first. It might have blown away." He carefully took out the folded sheet.

"Dear Kids:

Here is dinner money for tonight, tomorrow, and Wednesday. We want Laurie to save her strength for The Big Day!

Lots of love,
Mom.

P.S. Why don't you each take a turn at choosing a restaurant? Make it Danny's turn tonight.

Immediately, Laurie began weeping; it was her usual custom to weep on all such occasions.

Keith hurriedly said, "Let's go." And Danny said, "Let's go to The Village Smithburger. It's my favorite restaurant."

"Suits me," Keith replied. "You're the boss."

Laurie dabbed at her eyes. "Me, too," she said in a small voice that sounded very much like Tracy's.

The three started across to the air-terminal parking lot, and Keith patted Laurie's shoulder. "Cheer up," he said. "It's only a twelve-pound turkey, and you can rest up from now until Thursday."

Laurie half-giggled through her tears.

"And I'll put the dishes in the dishwasher for you after Thanksgiving Dinner," Danny rashly promised.

Laurie smiled at her brothers. "Sometimes I'm *very* fond of you—both. I can't understand it!"

The Village Smithburger was one of the most popular places in town, and on a Friday or Saturday night it was packed with Keith's and Laurie's friends. But tonight only a few people were scattered around the big room.

"Hi, Keith," the waitress Virgie Thomas smiled. "How's my classmate? Hi, Laurie and Danny." She handed menus around. "What brings you here on a dull Monday night?"

"We're keeping house," Laurie explained. "Mother's off to Florida for a week with Chris and Tracy."

"Yeah," Danny laughed. "And this is our home away from home. It says so here on the menu."

Virgie smiled and took up her pad and pencil. "Okay. What'll it be, Mr. Partridge?"

100

"The Smithburger luxury-special," Danny said promptly. "And a chocolate shake—thick."

Virgie took all three orders. "Is the TV too loud?" she asked. "I can have it turned down."

"I was going to ask you to turn it up," Keith replied. "It's almost newstime, and I'd like to hear the sportscast."

"Done!" Virgie said, and hurried off.

The newscast had already started when she returned with a tray heaped with Danny Partridge's favorite food. As she began to set down the plates, the announcer said, "A bulletin has just been handed to me." He paused, and all the Partridges looked up at the TV screen. "Miss Anabel Penland," the announcer continued, "said to be one of the world's ten wealthiest women and controlling stockholder of the giant Penland Chemical Company, has disappeared in this city. This fact became known when her chauffeur, Remi Rzcki (I believe I have that right)—R-z-c-k-i, reported to the police that he had called for Miss Penland at a hospital around 10:30 this morning. He stated that she had asked him to stop by a drugstore on an errand for her. When he returned to the street about four minutes later, the car and its single occupant were gone. He was jumped by two masked men . . . One moment please." The announcer paused.

"Another bulletin on this story has just come in. A plum-colored Rolls-Royce, registered in the name of Anabel Penland, has just been located by the police. Police report no trace of violence having taken place in the car. And so far, no trace of the vanished Miss Penland. As yet, there is no report of a ransom demand. More on the 11:00 newscast."

Keith and Laurie stared at each other. "Oh, how dreadful!" Laurie exclaimed. "Poor Pam!"

"Poor Miss Penland," Keith said.

But Danny didn't say a word. His golden freckles stood out like corn flakes in milk. Robert's words rang in his ears: *"and then they'd start on us."*

"Ought we to telephone them?" Laurie asked. "I mean—would it be—I mean—"

"Sure, telephone," Keith replied.

"Or maybe we should go right over, instead," Laurie suggested. "That would let Pam know we were really concerned."

Danny clutched his milkshake glass. "We've got to get them out of that house. They can't stay there. Somebody might—" he stopped.

"Might what?" Keith asked.

How Danny heartily wished he hadn't promised to keep any secrets! He wished he could go straight to Mr. Crandall and get him to call out the National Guard, or something. Robert must really be in danger now. Danny swallowed and looked up at Keith. "Well—how would you like to be in that gloomy old house when you've just had news like that?" he asked.

"Danny's right. We should at least ask," Laurie agreed. "Maybe it would get their minds off things."

"How can you get your mind off a thing like having your only living relative murdered?" Danny blurted out.

Laurie and Keith stared at him. "Who said anything about murder, Danny?" Keith asked. "Miss Penland is a very rich woman. She's been kidnapped, and a ransom will be paid—and, well, that will be that. Anyhow, we'll drive over there and see them—if they want to see us."

"Now, remember, Danny," Laurie warned as Keith swung the station wagon off the street at the Penland driveway. "We're not *visiting* Pam and Robert—

we're just *calling* on them. We'll ask if we can help in any way, and then we'll leave."

"What if they say they want us to help?" Danny asked. "Do we leave anyhow?"

"Don't be silly," Laurie answered. "How could we help?"

"Then why are we asking? Besides, I thought you were inviting them to come over to our house."

Keith pulled up in front of the mansion. "We'll wait in the car, Danny. Laurie, you go and see how things are."

"Well!" Danny exclaimed indignantly. "What will Robert think about me not showing up? *I'm* his friend."

"Sure you are," Keith replied. "That's why it's better if you stay here. Maybe he's all upset. Anyhow, you'll be seeing him tomorrow—if not sooner."

"I'll signal you, Danny," Laurie said, opening the car door. "If Robert wants to see you, I'll wave. How's that?"

"Okay."

The boys watched Laurie as she went up the steps, rang the bell, and waited. They saw Karya open the door. Laurie stepped inside, and the door was closed behind her.

"Now how can she signal?" Danny asked disgustedly.

"I don't think she'll stay long," Keith answered. "Just watch."

"I sort of wanted to go in," Danny said. "I've never been anywhere downstairs, except in the hall, of course."

In the mansion, Laurie sat alone in the living room and waited. In a moment, Mrs. Gruff came hurrying in. She was wringing her hands, and when she spoke, her voice trembled. "Oh, Laurie, my dear," she exclaimed. "I've been trying to call you people for the last half-hour. I'm so worried! I tried to call the Crandalls, too, but no one answered."

Laurie's heart brimmed with sympathy. Mrs. Gruff looked as though she might collapse any second. And Laurie found herself saying, "Why don't you sit down, Mrs. Gruff? I'm sure everything is going to be all right." She patted Mrs. Gruff's fat shoulder comfortingly and led her to a chair.

"You're so kind," Mrs. Gruff gasped. "The children are so lucky to have the Partridge Family as friends." She dabbed at her eyes.

"Now how can we help?" Laurie asked.

Mrs. Gruff hesitated. "Well, that's why I was trying to reach you, dear. You see, I'm just *dreading* newspaper reporters. Probably that senseless Remi has already told the police that Miss Penland's young relatives are here." She clasped her hands again and groaned. "Oh, I just should have gone to New York with him. I would never have allowed harm to come to that poor dear soul! It's all so terrible."

"Don't blame yourself," Laurie said quickly. "And as for reporters bothering you—well, I suppose they might. But why couldn't Pam and Robert come to our house? We've plenty of room, and we'd love to have them. And nobody would ever think of looking there for them."

Mrs. Gruff stopped weeping. "I was going to ask that very thing, dear. But Pamela and Robert were set against my doing it. They said they didn't want to involve anyone else." Again she dabbed at her eyes.

"Nonsense!" Laurie exclaimed. "Suppose I run up and talk with Pam?"

Relief flooded Mrs. Gruff's voice. "Oh, would you, dear? It would be so kind."

Out in the car, both Keith and Danny were growing impatient. "Leave it to Laurie to take forever," Keith muttered.

"Yeah," Danny said gloomily. "She and Pam must be talking over Great-aunt Anabel's life history or something."

Just then the door opened, and Laurie came hurrying down the steps. "Keith, take Danny and me home, will you? I'll get Mother's room ready for Pam, and Robert can have Chris's room. Then you can drive back here and pick them up with their luggage."

Quickly she explained Mrs. Gruff's fears about reporters. "And the poor thing is so upset! My heart just ached for her. But I had quite a time convincing Pam that she and Robert should come over."

"What about Robert?" Danny asked. "I should think your heart would be aching for *him*. After all, *Mrs*. Gruff's great-aunt hasn't been kidnapped."

"Well, she feels responsible, and she's worried," Laurie replied.

"Danny—will you stop worrying so much about Robert?" exclaimed Keith. "He's no worse off than Pam—or Mrs. Gruff."

"That's all you know about it," Danny thought angrily.

Why *ever* had he given Robert his word?

Chapter Thirteen

☐ Just as Laurie and Danny climbed out of the station wagon in their own driveway, Barry Crandall came sprinting up in the dark.

"Hey! Did you hear about Miss Penland?" he called out, even before he reached them. "Man! I'll bet my dad is having fits if he had his car radio on!"

"His *car* radio?" Laurie asked.

Barry went up the walk with them. "Yeah. This must be grandparents-bad-luck week. Just after you kids started off for the airport with your mother, Dad telephoned and told Mom to throw some things in a suitcase. My Granddad Crandall had some kind of attack. Anyhow, away they went, and here I am. I thought maybe you'd insist on my staying all night with you."

"It looks like the whole neighborhood is going to be staying over here all night!" Danny said cheerfully.

"Danny!" Laurie exclaimed.

"As a matter of fact," Keith began, as he unlocked the front door, "no—we won't insist."

"Keith!" Laurie exploded. "What a thing to say!"

Keith flashed on the hall light. "Laurie, will you please stop being so shocked? Barry isn't." He turned to Barry. "How about my going over to your place instead? Pam and Robert Smith are coming over here.

Mrs. Gruff's afraid reporters will be at their place. It isn't that we don't have plenty of room, but—"

"Sure," Barry said quickly. "Say no more! With all that gloom and doom going on, who needs a house-party? But you don't have to baby-sit for me, Keith. Maybe Laurie would feel better if the man of the house stayed home."

"Goodness, no!" Laurie said quickly. "We'll have Danny, won't we? I think it's a good idea, Keith. Why don't you take Barry with you back to Penlands, and I'll get busy here?" She turned to Danny. "Do you think Robert would rather bunk in with you, or have Chris's room? Don't answer that. We'll give him his choice." She flew up the stairs.

Usually any passerby could see the Partridge's big living room window glow cheerfully at night, but this evening the blinds were tilted shut. Pam and Robert needed privacy, and blocking the view into the house was the first thing to be done.

In the living room, Keith passed around sodas. "Danny, you and Robert had better turn in pretty soon," he said. "It's a school night same as usual."

Danny turned bright-red. "Not until after the newscast," he answered quickly. "Besides, I don't get this, Keith. Who ever heard of sending the man of the house to bed?"

For once, Laurie was on Danny's side. "*I* never heard of it," she agreed. "And Robert certainly wants to hear the late news."

Barry, who'd had very little to say, suddenly spoke up. "You know—I've been thinking. For a nervous old lady, Mrs. Gruff is pretty sharp—I mean, thinking ahead about reporters." He turned to Pam. "Do you suppose she maybe thought those people who work for you are in on some kind of plot?"

"What do you mean?" Pam asked, her eyes widening.

110

"Well—supposing she might think that Remi's story isn't true? He's the same nationality as the others, isn't he? Maybe Mrs. Gruff doesn't trust any of them, and that's why she's so nervous."

Pam flushed. "Robert and I are 'the same nationality,' as you put it, too."

"But I thought you were English!" Laurie said in surprise.

"Why don't you tell them, Pam?" Robert said quietly. "Danny knows. I told him."

There was utter silence across the room—and then Pam spoke. "I guess I'd better begin with Remi, as you asked about him first. Robert and I aren't sure about Remi at all. And we're not absolutely sure which side Remi and Karya are on. But we know which side Otto Karel and his wife are on—ours. They worked for our mother and father for years. In fact, they fled from Carpathia with our parents. Robert and I would trust them with our lives."

Danny looked from one puzzled face to another around the room. "I'll bet you don't know where Carpathia is," he said. "And I'll bet there's something you'd never guess even if you did know. It just happens that Robert is *prince* of it." He looked at Robert. "I hope that was okay to tell?" Robert nodded.

"I told Danny yesterday, Pam," he said. "With Great-aunt about to come home, I thought I might as well. Besides, he never did believe our name was Smith."

From there on, the explanation moved swiftly. It was nearly the same story that Robert had confided in Danny, except that Pam didn't say a word about the Penland Chemical Company possibly falling into the hands of the government of Carpathia. And Danny nearly forgot that she omitted it as he listened, spellbound, to Pam's account of her parents' violent endings, which Robert had not told.

111

"After Mother's fatal accident last year in England, it was discovered that the brake cylinder of her car had been tampered with, and that it was certain somebody had meant her to plunge over the cliff. There was a lot in the newspapers about it, and they dug up the story of Father's death in Switzerland the year before. At first, everybody had thought it was a skiing accident. And of course it was—only someone had tampered with the left ski binding so that it loosened." She hesitated. "Well, I needn't go on about it. But anyhow, that is why the name 'Smith' seemed a better name to use than Radiczncek—our own name. It had been in the newspapers so much."

"And harder to say, too," Danny added helpfully.

"No wonder Mrs. Gruff flutters around," Keith said. "She probably heard the whole story from your great-aunt and then felt she had to stand guard over you."

Barry looked at his watch. "It's newstime," he said.

Danny sprang to turn on the TV, and Pam said to Barry, "Do you suppose your father knew the real story? I wasn't sure, but when he called us 'Smith,' I took it for granted we should keep our real name a secret."

Barry shrugged. "I'd never know. Dad keeps his clients' affairs pretty secret."

"Listen!" Danny exclaimed, nodding toward the TV screen.

What followed on the newscast was mostly a recap of the earlier news story. "Still no clues and no ransom note," the announcer said. "But we have learned that the deserted Rolls-Royce was found along the heavily traveled New Jersey Turnpike. Police have stated that a transfer to another car must have been made—and within plain sight of hundreds of passing motorists. Police have asked that anyone who may have seen the transfer take place to please come forward with any possible information. And now to the weather—"

In Barry Crandall's room, Barry reached up and snapped off the light. A minute or so passed, and then he said, "Keith, are you asleep?"

"No. Why?"

"I just wanted to ask you something. Do you believe in astrology?"

"Why?" Keith asked back. He turned his head toward the window and looked out at the frosty twinkling stars. "Do you see something up there that I don't?"

"Probably not," Barry replied, thumping his pillow. "But I was just thinking—your grandmother, my granddad, and Miss Penland. They must all be about the same age, I guess, and they've all had bad luck one way or another. I wonder if all three were born under the same sign?"

Keith groaned. "Go to sleep, will you?"

In Danny's room the light by Robert's bunk clicked on. "What's up?" Danny squinted as he watched Robert go over to the chair where he'd left his slacks.

"I just remembered something," Robert said. "The envelope we found yesterday. I forgot to read it."

Danny sat up. "Well, it couldn't be anything very important, I guess. But what does it say?"

Robert took out a folded sheet. "It's typed," he said. "And this is rather odd—it's addressed to Mrs. Gruff and it's postmarked 'New York, New York,' but—" he paused and swallowed.

"But *what?*"

"Well, I never knew she could read a foreign language."

"Is that all?" Danny exclaimed. "Lots of people can.

113

Maybe its from her old father who used to live in Germany or something."

"How about it's being from her old father who used to live in Carpathia?" Robert asked. "What would you think of *that?* Listen to this. It doesn't start out with a 'dear anybody'—it just begins: 'The holiday, Thanksgiving, the Americans celebrate—may it have real meaning for you. We wait to hear.' "

Danny leaned forward. "Let me see it." He looked at the envelope and then at the note. "They don't match," he said. "See, the paper's different. I get it! Probably Otto or somebody dropped it, and Mrs. Gruff stuck it in this envelope to save it for him and forgot to give it back."

"And then went up to the turret room and dropped it herself?" Robert asked. "Doesn't sound right to me."

"Well, it's possible," Danny argued. "Probably she explored up there one time while you kids were at school. Man! I would have! And remember—she doesn't have anything to do but sit around all day."

"That's so," Robert said thoughtfully. "And another thing—she's been with Great-aunt for years. She'd hardly have had much chance to get acquainted with the Carpathian language, would she?"

He went back to his bunk. "Well, goodnight again," he said, sighing. He snapped off the light.

In the dark Danny tried to think of something cheerful to say to his friend. But what can you say cheerful to a guy who's wondering if his only living relative's been murdered—and wondering if he'll be next? he asked himself.

He shivered and pulled the blanket tight around his ears.

Chapter Fourteen

☐ Laurie was counting out breakfast eggs when Pam came into the kitchen. "Hi," she said. "What do I do? I'm pretty good at buttering toast."

Laurie laughed. "I've a feeling it's going to be every man for himself around here. How do you like your eggs?"

"Very much," Pam grinned. "Why don't we just scramble them? I could do that."

"Great. Then I'll do the juice," Laurie replied.

"Hi, girls!" Keith and Barry came into the kitchen.

"Your cooking lured us over," Barry said. "What do you want me to do? Set the table?"

There was a sharp rap at the kitchen door.

"Why, it's Karya!" Pam cried. "What could be wrong?" She hurried to open the door.

Karya spoke rapidly in a language the others did not understand. Then she smiled and nodded at everybody. "It is not to worry," she said.

But Pam spoke worriedly. "What hospital is it, Karya? I must call."

Karya's face changed. She clapped a hand to her forehead. "I do not look! I do not ask!" Then she said, "But it is white ambulance I see and light on top turns."

"What's happened," Keith, Barry, and Laurie asked together.

"It's Mrs. Gruff," Pam said. "Karya told me that Mrs. Gruff woke her at four o'clock this morning to say that she had already called for an ambulance herself, and she was all dressed and ready to go to the hospital. She said it was just 'the flutters' and not to worry. And she said Karya mustn't tell us until breakfast time. Isn't that just like Mrs. Gruff? Worrying herself to pieces and never wanting to be a worry herself!"

"Finding the right hospital won't be a problem," Keith said. "There are only two in town. I'll go call right now."

Robert and Danny were in the kitchen by the time Keith came back, and he was frowning. "I hate to tell you, Pam—but Mrs. Gruff isn't in either hospital. I—I guess she's just *vanished*."

Pam clutched at the back of a kitchen chair. "Call the police," she said in a thin voice. "And tell them—tell them to find that ambulance and *arrest everybody in it. It's been Mrs. Gruff all along!*"

The only person who seemed able to concentrate on breakfast was Danny. He ate silently while Pam read the note Robert had given her, and then he listened carefully while Robert told the others how it had been discovered.

"But I don't understand," Pam said. "What connection would it have with all this that has been going on? The note just sounds like a greeting from a friend."

Danny pushed back his chair and stood up. "I know where your Great-aunt Anabel is," he announced.

"Danny," Laurie said sharply. "Don't show off. This means too much to Pam and Robert."

"Besides," said Keith, "isn't it about time for you to catch the school bus, Dan?"

Danny's face went into a bright-pink and then on to a dark-red. His fists balled together, and his eyes dampened from sheer rage. "That's about what I'd expect you to say," he exploded, his voice rising. "I should have kept my promise to *never* tell this family anything—*ever!*"

Barry Crandall had seen Danny Partridge's gunpowder temper explode before, but the Smiths—or Radicznceks—almost forgot their own problems as they watched a suddenly enraged Danny slam his chair up to the table, then race out of the kitchen.

Robert started to follow. "Wait, Robert," Keith said. "Danny doesn't stay mad long. Between us, Laurie and I sort of piled it on, I guess. I'll go fix things up with him."

As he pushed back his chair, the front door slammed loudly. Keith shrugged. "I guess not. Danny's left for school."

But Danny Partridge had not left for school. He was running as fast as he could—straight to the front door of the Penland mansion.

"Why Master Danny! Good morning it is!" Karya smiled.

Danny almost pushed past her. "Excuse me!" he muttered, and scarcely stopping, he raced up the stairs.

Karya's jaw dropped. She looked after the disappearing Danny, then hurried to the back of the hall. "Otto, Otto!" she called.

By the time Otto and Karya, with Mrs. Karel following, reached the second floor, Danny was already on the third—and tugging with all his might at the heavy oak door leading to the left-side turret room. It was locked. He raced back to the right-side door.

Locked. "I knew it would be locked by now!" he exclaimed. "I just *knew* it!"

He started to rush back along the main hallway, and then he saw Otto and the two women walking hurriedly toward him. "Keys!" he shouted. "Get the keys!"

Otto stared. "No keys. What wrong is?"

"Then get an axe!" Danny shouted again. "An *axe*. Please!"

Otto didn't budge. He stared down at the red-faced, excited Danny, astonished. But Karya stepped forward. "Master Danny—you scare us. What for the axe?" She put a light hand on his shoulder.

He looked into her worried eyes, and he could almost feel his hot rage cool. But when he tried to speak in normal tones, his voice shook. "Robert's Great-aunt Anabel—" he said. "I think she's locked up in one of these rooms." He pointed upward.

Otto, his wife, and Karya stood frozen, and all three stared as though they were sure the boy from next door had suddenly lost his senses. Then Otto slowly shook his head. "Is not my door, young boy. You go home now. Nobody here."

Danny pushed past them all, and raced down the two flights of stairs. The three followed him. "Where's the telephone?" he shouted back. "I'll call Robert."

By the time Karya had hurried down the last steps and led Danny to the phone, he was so excited he could hardly remember his own telephone number. "If anybody'd believed me!" he said to himself, amazed at his own feelings. "Why, I started out being as cool as a cucumber—and then nobody would listen to me."

Keith answered the phone. "I want to speak to

Robert," Danny said loudly, wasting no time in even saying "hello."

"Robert? Say, Danny—where are you?" Keith asked.

"I'm next door," Danny shouted again, "and I'm in a hurry."

"Next door?" Keith exclaimed. "What are you doing next door?"

"Going crazy," Danny said angrily. "Keith, *please!* Get Robert for me."

"Well, okay," Keith said. "But you'd better explain later why you're not on the bus, and it better be *good.*"

Chapter Fifteen

☐ Within two minutes after Danny had hung up, Robert came bursting, coatless, through the hedge. He raced across the grounds, followed by all of the others.

Danny waited at the door for all of them, with Otto and the two women standing anxiously behind him.

"Get the axe, Otto," Robert panted as he raced up the front steps.

Otto disappeared immediately, and eight people rushed up the stairs—only to stand waiting at the turret-room door for his return.

"That's some door," Barry said. "Are you sure the keys aren't around, Pam? It seems a shame to hack through it."

Pam shook her head. "Mrs. Gruff had them," she replied in a stiff voice.

As they heard Otto's heavy steps come along the main hallway, Laurie said, "I wish I'd put on a coat." Her teeth chattered. "It's freezing up here."

Nobody made any reply. They all stepped back to make way for Otto.

He glanced at the narrow hall space. "Get coats," he said. "Very good idea. All get coats. Much room I need to swing axe. Time it will take."

Nobody lost any time in returning to watch Otto's

progress. But as nobody had a very clear view, the sudden silence when the blows stopped was almost startling. Danny and Robert both stepped forward, but Otto blocked them. He bowed to Robert. "No—it is for me to look. I go."

He leaned the axe against the wall and pulled at the notch he had cut out around the heavy lock. As the door swung back, an even colder draft of air struck them. Slowly Otto climbed the steps. There was absolute silence behind him, and the group listened to his footsteps crossing the floor above.

"She must be there!" Pam whispered, her voice shaking. "He's taking so *long*."

Otto called down from the top step. "She lives. Call doctor. I bring down. Make hot tea. Get blankets. Freezing here."

"I'll call," Barry said. "Where's the phone?"

He hurried away, the servants and Laurie following him.

Danny stood with Robert and Pam at the foot of the stairs, but Keith pulled him back. "Danny, she's *their* family," Keith said. "That was some brainstorm you had. But now, come on—we're in the way."

Danny groaned. "Somebody's been sending me to some other place ever since this day started," he said. "But okay."

Nobody went to school that morning, and nearly everybody had some special thing to do. Pam talked with the doctor outside of her great-aunt's door.

Barry telephoned the news to his father, and Laurie waited her turn to call Shirley in Florida. Keith helped Karya to give her story to the police about Mrs. Gruff's leaving in an ambulance. And Robert went to the kitchen to talk with Mrs. Karel about preparing a huge lunch to celebrate finding Great-aunt Anabel alive.

Thanks to Danny, Miss Penland had been found before the chill of the unheated room threatened her life. But now, the unsung hero of the morning had nothing to do but look out the window for reporters that never arrived. Finally, Keith walked into the living room. "Say, Danny—how did you get this all figured out?" he asked.

"Simple," Danny said airily. "I just kept adding two and two. And then at breakfast, I was looking at Pam and Robert, and I suddenly thought about how Mrs. Gruff would hardly let them out of her sight. Then all of a sudden, just when something *really* happens, what does she do? She gets them out of the *house*. And of course there were several other things—" he broke off and stared at Keith. "What's the matter, Keith? What's wrong?"

Keith stared right through Danny, and then without answering he began to race out into the hall and back toward the kitchen.

"What's the *matter?*" Danny puffed, catching up.

"Otto!" Keith called. "Otto! Get the axe!"

A dizzy feeling suddenly swept over Danny. "I must be dreaming!" he told himself. "It's Keith's voice, but that's *my* line!"

It was no dream—and for the second time that morning, the sound of Otto's axe rang through the deserted third floor. The scene that followed was almost a replay of Great-aunt Anabel's rescue. Otto came down the steps of the second-turret room, carefully holding another elderly woman in his arms.

"But how—?" Pam whispered, her hand at her throat. "Who is it?"

127

"Mrs. Gruff," Keith replied grimly. "The *real* Mrs. Gruff."

By the time they sat down for lunch, the household had calmed down. Great-aunt Anabel was peacefully sleeping, warm and safe now in spite of the drug she had been given by her captors, and the true Mrs. Gruff was safely in the hospital. She would be all right eventually, but the doctor said she was very frail. "This woman has been half-starved for weeks," he had said. "What happened here?"

"We don't know the whole story," Pam had replied. "We hope she'll be able to tell us part of it."

One thing they were sure of—the ambulance that had taken the fake Mrs. Gruff away had brought the two elderly women to the Penland mansion. And now, at the table, Pam was quivering in anger.

"When I think of how I've felt so *sorry* for that Mrs. Gruff—I mean the wrong Mrs. Gruff—I could just explode."

"Don't waste time thinking about it," Keith advised. "What I'm wondering about is how—"

"Telephone, Miss Pam," Karya said from the doorway.

While she was away from the table, Danny said, "I think I know what happened."

This time nobody told him to stop showing off.

"I think the police will find the ambulance somewhere," he began. "It was probably stolen from some hospital. And I think that on the Jersey Turnpike when your Aunt Anabel was kidnapped, Mrs. Gruff —the real one—was already in the car that came along. And I'll bet she was drugged."

Pam came back to the table. "Two pieces of news. They found the ambulance. And where do you suppose? Parked by a hospital. It had been stolen from another hospital."

"Danny, you're a prophet!" Robert exclaimed. "Danny just said that," he said to Pam.

Pam nodded, "He did? Well, the other thing—the police say they have leads on the men, but that they think Mrs. Gruff—the fake one—got away to Europe."

"Already!" Laurie gasped. "But if she went to Europe, she wasn't planning to ask for ransom money then. Why! What she meant was plain *murder!* If it hadn't been for Danny, those two poor old ladies would have died up there in the cold before anybody found them!"

Danny looked at Pam and Robert. Neither said a word that would explain that they thought murder *was* intended.

Pam only nodded. "We'll know sometime, I expect. Anyhow, the police said that a woman, with a Carpathian passport and answering her description, boarded a plane this morning headed for Europe. They said she probably wouldn't have been noticed, but she got into a loud argument in some foreign language with two men. The airline people said she complained they were bothering her. Anyhow, whoever she was, she got on the plane. And she's gone."

It seemed impossible that the morning they had just been through could be followed by an afternoon of school-as-usual—and then two solid hours of rock-music practice. But that was exactly what happened.

"Danny," Laurie said, as she gathered up their music, "how would you like to go back to The Village Smithburger for dinner tonight?"

Danny grinned. "Laurie, do you realize that only this morning you were a *cruel* sister? How do you switch your personalities so fast?"

Keith stretched his arms and dropped down on the couch. "You know, I was just thinking—about those notes. The notes sent to Pam and the one we got."

"What note did we get?" Danny asked.

Keith grinned. "Can it be something around here escaped your eagle eye?" But he explained.

"You should have mentioned this to me earlier," Danny said. "Who knows? Maybe I could have solved this case faster."

"Oh, Danny!" Laurie groaned. "You're impossible!"

"I could have compared the typing," Danny replied calmly. "Maybe the same person who typed the note we found in the turret room typed those notes. Anyhow, I'm sure the police would be interested."

Keith jumped up. "Danny's right. I'd better call Pam and tell her not to throw it away."

"I'll bet it's still right on our kitchen table," Laurie said. "We left in such a hurry—oh! *dishes!* Keith, Danny! The breakfast dishes! Oh, wow! How does Mom keep up with this routine?"

As all three headed for the kitchen, the telephone rang. Keith picked it up. "Oh—hi, Pam," they heard him say.

Laurie and Danny went on to the kitchen. "I wonder if Robert's going to want to talk with me?" Danny said.

"I'd bet on it," Laurie smiled.

But she was wrong. Keith hung up the phone and came out to the kitchen. "No late developments," he said.

"I'll bet that the government of Carpathia will be plenty mad when they discover no dead bodies are reported," Danny said cheerfully.

Laurie looked puzzled. "But how could they have expected them to be found?" she asked. "Oh! I get it!

In a couple of weeks they could have had one of those two mysterious men who were at the airport with the fake Mrs. Gruff notify the police and tell them to look. I'll bet that's it. Then Pam and Robert would be declared the heirs and—" her eyes widened in horror. *"Then they'd be next!"*

"I figured that out, too," Keith said. "And what bothers me—Miss Penland isn't going to live forever even if nobody ever kidnaps her again. Then what happens to Pam and Robert? Maybe some relatives on the Carpathian side of the family will make the kids go back there someday because they'd own most of Penland Chemical. Wow! That could mean that the company might be owned by an Iron Curtain satellite!"

Danny put the juice glasses into the dishwasher. "I think their troubles are going to be over," he said. "I've advised Robert to get legal advice."

"You mean you couldn't help him out yourself?" Keith asked, his eyes twinkling.

Danny ignored that. "What else did Pam tell you—or was that it?" he asked.

"Oh!" Keith replied. "Glad you asked. She says that Miss Penland wants us to have dinner there tomorrow night. She wants to personally thank her rescuer."

Danny flushed. "I sure hope she doesn't want to give me a handsome reward—say like a million dollars. I couldn't take it on account of my friendship with Robert."

"That's right—you couldn't." Keith's voice was serious, but his emerald eyes flashed with fun.

"Something smaller, do you think?" Danny asked. "Say like a thousand?"

Keith shook his head.

"Five hundred?"

Again Keith shook his head.

"Well, I wouldn't go under two-fifty," Danny announced.

"Danny Partridge," Laurie exploded. "You *are* impossible."

"Now don't change your personality again," Danny grinned. "I like you better the way you were a minute ago."

Laurie only half-smiled back. "Then run upstairs and change your shirt before I change my personality. Or maybe I'll take back my offer on The Village Smithburger.

Even to Danny, his bedroom was a mess. His things and Robert's half-unpacked belongings were strewn all over.

"Man!" he thought. "That first Mrs. Gruff must have planned for Robert to stay here for *weeks!* All the hangers in the closet are used up."

Danny looked over Robert's clothes. There was one very British-looking gray suit, a navy jacket, and two pairs of slacks that were crowded in beside Danny's clothes.

Suddenly a light leaped into his eyes. He reached up, lifted the gray suit from the rack, and walked to the mirror with it. His eyes sparkled. "I'll have to ask Robert first," he said to himself. "But I'll bet he'll think it's a great idea."

Danny worked quickly, and loaded all of Robert's clothing but the gray suit into the suitcase. Then on the top he added a pair of his own corduroy slacks and a red turtleneck jersey. He snapped the bag shut. "Man! Will we fool Mrs. McAllister!"

"Hey, Keith," Danny called as he came thumping down the stairs with the heavy suitcase. "Could we drop this off at Robert's? I happen to know he needs some of this stuff for school tomorrow."

"That isn't a bad idea, Keith," Laurie said. "I could pack Pam's things, too. And then we could drop off both cases."

Just as they were going out the door, the telephone rang. "Probably Barry," Keith said. "I'll get it."

But it was Shirley Partridge—telling the kids to meet the five p.m. plane on Thanksgiving Day. "Grandma's just fine," she said. "And when she and Grandpa heard Laurie was fixing the turkey, they said we shouldn't miss it! So we're on our way Thursday. Now, lots of love, kids. See you soon."

At the Penland front door, Danny managed only a quick conversation with Robert—but that was all that he needed. Laurie, waving up at Pam from the station wagon, wondered what on earth the boys had found that was so funny. Robert seemed to be hooting with laughter, and when Danny came back to the car, his eyes were twinkling with mischief.

"Well, I'll never know, I guess," Laurie said to herself. "But it's time those kids had some fun!"

Wednesday morning at school was a complete success. Danny managed Robert's British accent well enough to fool Mrs. McAllister. Robert's American accent was not as good, but he managed to keep a straight face when Mrs. McAllister said, "Why on earth are you talking in that strange way, Danny?"

"I'm trying to develop a British accent, Mrs. McAllister," Robert replied. "In case I ever go to England, I should prefer to talk like a native."

The disguised Danny tried not to split with laughter—and that was the way the morning went.

At noon, all of East Valley Elementary went rushing out to the yellow school buses. Robert looked around for Danny.

"Hey! Danny! Danny! Over here!" Robert looked around. It was Keith, driving the station wagon. Laurie, Pam, and Barry were with him.

Robert didn't hesitate to continue in his role of being Danny. He ran to the car and hopped in.

"Where's Robert?" Pam asked.

Robert couldn't trust his voice. He motioned toward the school bus ahead, and then went into a sudden fit of coughing.

"Oh, well. Let's go, Keith," Pam said. "We'll beat him home."

At the Penland mansion, Robert jumped out with Pam. "The joke's over," he said, grinning.

"Hey, Danny!" Keith said. "Where're you going?"

Robert doubled over laughing. "I'm *Robert*," he gasped. "We've fooled *everybody*."

"So that's what you two were up to last night!" Laurie exclaimed. "I should have known from the gleam in Danny's eye that something was going on!"

Pam laughed. "Well—thanks for the ride. And we'll see you tonight."

As Keith pulled to a stop before turning back into the street, the school bus pulled up to the curb.

"Let's just wave to Danny when he gets off and then drive the other way," Keith said.

"Oh, that would be mean," Laurie replied. "After all, they were just having a little fun for a change."

"Okay," Keith grinned. "But I think your sense of humor is underdeveloped!"

They watched three neighborhood children jump off the bus. The door snapped shut, and the bus rolled on its way.

"But where's Danny?" Laurie asked.

"Missed the bus," Keith said gloomily. "We'll have to go all the way back."

But Danny Partridge was not to be found anywhere—anywhere in town, that is. And no wonder!

Gagged and tied, Danny, still wearing Robert's suit, was lying on the floor of a car, speeding along the expressway—which way, or where to, he didn't know!

Chapter Sixteen

☐ Danny had come racing out to the buses just in time to see Keith pull away in the station wagon. "Blawst!" he exclaimed in his most Englishy accent, just in case any classmate might hear him.

"Master Robert! Master Robert!" a voice cried.

Danny looked around. Across the street was a long black car, and who should be shouting from it but Remi! Danny waited for the crossover light to turn green, and then he shot across the street. As he neared the car, he could see that two men were sitting in the back seat. A warning went off in the back of his mind, but he ignored it. The masquerade was too much fun. "I wonder if I can fool Remi?" he thought. "I'll bet I can."

Remi reached over and opened the front door. "Jump in—here beside me, Master Robert."

Danny hopped in. He nodded to the two men. "I say, Remi, when did you get back? I guess they've told you all about Great-aunt being rescued and that Mrs. Gruff was a fake, haven't they?"

Remi nodded. "I hear. Yesterday, police in New York City tell me. I rush back."

"Where's our Rolls?" Danny asked.

"In New York City garage. Repaired it is being," Remi explained. He swung the black car to the right.

"Errance I do first, Master Robert. Take friends home. Then to house we go."

"Very well," Danny said grandly. "Drive on."

It was the last thing he had to say for quite some time. They passed by long stretches of vacant lots, and just as he was wondering where Remi's friends might live, a scarf was suddenly thrown over his head. Before he could count to two, his arms were jerked back and tied. Then Danny Partridge felt himself being dragged up and over the back seat, his legs wildly kicking—but not for long. In another second, his ankles were tied as tight as his wrists, and he was pushed down to the car floor. Then—worst of all—a blanket was dropped over him.

Remi slowed and stopped the car. The men in the back seat stepped out and moved to the front, and Danny was left—furious as he had ever been in his life!

As the miles wore on, Danny stopped being angry. He realized they must be driving along the expressway, and for the first time, he began to worry about where he was being taken. Snatches of conversation reached him from the front seat. "Why didn't I learn Carpathian?" he asked himself disgustedly.

He was sure it must be after dark when he felt the car slow and turn off the expressway. After about ten long minutes, it slid to a stop. Rough hands bundled the heavy blanket around him. Then, like an extralarge bag of groceries, he was lifted out and carried up a few steps. A door slammed, and he realized they had entered a building. Then more steps and another door—and Danny Partridge was dumped onto a lumpy bed.

The blanket was jerked off. The scarf was pushed down from his face, and, in the glare of an unshaded light bulb, Danny looked again into Remi's face.

"And so, young Rupert," Remi sneered. "Too bad it is that you leave not your relative to die. Now you find out if she likes you. It will cost her much! To Carpathia you go!"

It was on the tip of Danny's tongue to fling Remi's mistake right in his face. And he almost said, "But I couldn't make a *dime* for Carpathia. I'm Danny Partridge!"

But something in Remi's coldly glowing eyes stopped him. Danny suddenly realized he wouldn't be *worth* a dime if Remi learned that such a mistake had been made. Besides, they'd go back for Robert. So he concentrated on playing the part and tried his best to think of something princely to say—which was quite hard, considering he was flat on his back on a very uncomfortable bed. "You are a *varlet!*" he said in a chilly voice.

Remi frowned. He spoke rapidly and angrily in his own language. "Speak English while you are in this country!" Danny said sternly.

Remi slashed through the ties on Danny's wrists and ankles. He jerked him up and dragged him to the window. "Nobody to see. Nobody to hear. No need yelling."

With the bright light that dangled from the ceiling, everything outside was black as pitch. But Danny was sure nothing could have been seen anyhow; Remi would never have taken such a chance. He tried to look very haughty. "I shall yell *when* and *where* I please," he said firmly.

Remi stared at him. "Be careful, young prince," he said. "Do you wish your sister to join you? Tomorrow to plane we go. No trouble. The Lady Pamela—you wish not harm to come to her? No?"

Danny's goosebumps massed beneath his turtleneck sweater and the warm gray suit. He turned quickly away, lest Remi should see the fear that sprang in his eyes.

"Good boy," Remi said. "Will stay good boy. I have feeling."

Once Remi had left the room, locking the door as he left, Danny lost no time in looking around. The door looked heavy and the window was barred. There wasn't much to see—only an old table, a rusty alarm clock, and a rusty old gooseneck lamp that had no lightbulb.

He flung himself back down on the old bed, and right away old bedspring wires poked into his back. Carefully, he pushed himself up and off the bed. Then he lifted the edge of a dirty, thin mattress. "Man! It's a wonder I wasn't stabbed to death," he said to himself as he viewed the old coil springs that were toppled and rusty. "I think I'll demand a better bed."

At that moment, the key noisily turned in the door, and the two men Danny had last seen riding in the back seat of the car stepped into the room.

What happened next was nearly worse than being kidnapped! They jerked off his parka-hooded coat, flung off Robert's gray jacket, and peeled off his own white turtleneck sweater. Then they pushed and shoved Danny roughly between them along a dimly lit hall and into a dingy bathroom. Before Danny could even sputter, his entire head was dunked into a basin of water. And when they'd finished thumping and bumping his head and had handed him a towel, Danny Partridge looked up into a cracked mirror. What he saw made him as angry as he had ever been in his life! Inky black locks streamed wetly along his face. His red hair was gone!

Back at the Penland mansion, it was seven o'clock, and Miss Anabel Penland at her dining-room table was giving orders left and right. She seemed to be completely recovered, and, as Mr. Crandall had said, she wasn't nearly so old as the kids had imagined. Anyhow, she was strong and lively enough to take command like a general.

She looked around the table. "Now, Laurie—not only will swollen eyes not help—they'll be *dangerous*. You *must* pretend that Robert is your brother. It is of greatest importance that *nobody* discover the wrong boy has been kidnapped."

Then she turned to all of them. "From what you've told me about Daniel, I'm sure that right this minute he is pretending to be the Prince of Carpathia. He has probably been told that a ransom will be asked for the *return of the Prince* and he's *being* the Prince."

She turned to Keith. "This is nobody's fault but my own. How I could have imagined that Pamela and Robert could lead normal, everyday American lives, I can't guess. But that's behind me now, and all any of us must think about is Daniel's welfare. And that we shall do.

"You may be sure a ransom note will be received. There shall be no question of payment. It will be met. And I guarantee that Daniel is perfectly safe right this minute. Money, not a boy, is what those people want —and that they shall have if it takes every last cent I have. And now that brings me to the next step. The police are already on Remi's tracks, and—"

Karya entered the dining room carrying a long florist's box. "For you, ma'am," she said.

Miss Penland jerked off the strings and lifted the lid. Inside lay a bouquet of red roses. She ignored them and opened the card envelope. "Hmm! Sooner than I thought. Hear this: *You see our national colors. You know our demands must be met. You will hear them soon.*"

She sighed with relief. "Daniel, as I guessed, is

doing his part," she said. "They still do not know his true identity. Now come with me, Keith. There is much to be done, and I should like to speak to you alone."

But as she left the dining room, Miss Penland's heart was pounding. How long could she keep Keith Partridge believing that there was "much to be done," when the only thing to do was to wait for the ransom demand? Meantime, Danny's very life depended on no word leaking out that he was not the real Prince. And how could she face Shirley Partridge with the news that Danny had been kidnapped—and by as cruel a gang as Miss Penland could imagine! If Danny's real identity became known to his captors, she knew that not all the funds in the Penland Chemical Company could save him from his fate!

But fearful as the prospect was, it never occurred to Miss Penland nor the police that Danny Partridge's kidnappers would not wait out their ransom demand *in the United States*.

Chapter Seventeen

☐ Once again Danny was back in the dismal room. He rubbed the stained black towel over his head. "Man! I'll never live this down," he told himself angrily. "I'd sure hate to have my friends see me like this!" Then his eyes widened. "Oh, wow! What am I saying?"

Carefully, he sat down on the edge of the bed, trying to miss some of the loose bedsprings. He stared around. "What a dump!" he thought. "I'd almost rather we were leaving for Carpathia tonight!"

He had to swallow hard—the name "Carpathia" had stuck in his throat. "How'll I ever get out of this?" he asked himself.

Again the door key turned. This time it was Remi who appeared. He carried a small beaten-up metal tray, and on it were a container of milk, a paper-wrapped sandwich, and a candy bar. "We treat you like a prince? Yes?" Remi laughed nastily. "With the light on, you sleep. Better that way."

Danny said nothing, and Remi left, locking the door behind him.

It wasn't Danny's idea of a princely meal, but at least it gave him energy—and energy was what Danny Partridge was going to need! "Man! I hope this idea works," he muttered. "If it doesn't, I'm sunk."

For the next hour, Danny twisted and bent and tugged at the rustiest of the bedspring coils. As he worked each one loose, he speedily hid it beneath the rough blanket. Finally, his fingers and palms cut, scraped, and bleeding, Danny decided that one part of the plan was complete.

Then he started on the next step. He loaded every pocket in Robert's suit with bedspring coils and stuffed his outside coat pockets. Next, he jerked the worn cord from the goosneck lamp and laid it aside. Now it was time to "dress," and Danny went to work as quietly as possible. He pulled his turtleneck sweater back over his now dry—and black—hair. Working swiftly, he stuffed the old lamp under his sweater, then added the old alarm clock and a few bedspring coils. Next, he slipped the metal supper tray over everything. Last of all, he wrapped the lamp cord tightly around his waist and knotted it carefully. Now he was almost ready for tomorrow. He put on the gray jacket and found he could not fasten it across his new "bay window," so he slipped into his warm parka-hooded coat.

Then with the greatest care, Danny Partridge laid himself along the length of the sagging bed. He buttoned the coat, then pulled the blanket up over his sausage-like shape.

"Well, I've done all I can," he sighed. "I just hope I remember not to turn over all night."

He closed his eyes, and in the glare of the lamp bulb, fell fast asleep.

Next morning, while the sky was still gray, Danny was shaken awake. "Get up," Remi said in a hard voice. "Without breakfast you go. We leave now."

"Very well," Danny mumbled, even in his half-sleep trying to sound like a true Prince of Carpathia. "You may go."

"*I* may go!" Remi snarled. "*You* may go. And soon." He strode out of the room, this time not bothering to even close the door.

Danny carefully moved his stiff form out of bed. He could hardly wiggle his sore, stiff fingers. "It's a good thing I left my shoes on," he said to himself. "I'd never get them tied. Man! I didn't move all night. My circulation's stopped."

Remi gave Danny no more than five minutes to appear. He banged on the bathroom door. "Come! We go!"

When Danny stepped out into the hall, Remi scowled down at him. Now this time you sit straight in car. No noise. No trouble. Look—" He held out his hand, and in it Danny saw the glitter of a hypodermic needle. "One cry from you," Remi said, "and *this!*" He made a jabbing motion in the air. "We throw you away. Understand?"

Danny, his cut hands in his pockets, managed to keep his knees and his chest full of tools from rattling. He looked as coolly as possible at Remi. "Shall we leave?" he asked.

In a miraculously quiet way (considering the hardware he carried), Danny moved ahead of Remi down the hall, then on down the staircase. Stepping into the car would be the big test. Already he was regretting packing the bedsprings. They were scratching his chest and stomach.

"Some motel you have there," he said to Remi as he walked around the back of the car. "I imagine this is where you kept the real Mrs. Gruff. Do I get in front or in back?" he asked as he glanced at the license number.

Remi, annoyed as Danny had hoped he would be, almost lifted him off his feet and into the car. A plane, still climbing up from the airfield, helped to damp out the clanking sound.

It was not a long drive to the airport. In a cloudy dawn, Remi drove up to the terminal entrance. "I stay here," he said. "I keep the eye out for the Lady Pamela. You get out."

And before Danny, between the two men, had reached the terminal door, Remi had rushed on his way.

In the terminal, Danny expected to hear the amplifier calling out, "Flight to Carpathia—now boarding." Instead, it was, "flight to Rome—now boarding." His two jailers pushed him forward between them. One leaned down and spoke sternly to him in the same strange language Remi spoke.

"Speak English," Danny said coldly.

The man pressed his fingers around Danny's shoulders and shoved him forward in the straggling line going through the gates.

Danny's heart thumped. It was now or never. "Mom, Keith, Laurie, Chris, Tracy," he murmured to himself, "make them think I'm a skyjacker!" He squeezed his eyes shut. He neared the pass-through. "Mom, Keith, Laurie, Chris—" The men took out tickets and passports and shoved him forward. "Mom —Keith," Danny stumbled forward.

A hand closed on his shoulder. "If you'll come this way," a voice said politely. Danny looked up. Standing by him was a uniformed airlines official. "Stop them!" Danny exclaimed in almost a whisper. "Stop those men!" And unexpectedly, he sagged to the floor.

When Danny woke up, a nice nurse was swabbing his fingers and pressing Band-Aids around them. One hand was completely bandaged. "Hi," she said. "Who're you?"

Danny blinked. The weight that had been pressing

on his chest and stomach was gone. His turtleneck sweater was no longer stuffed out. "Who're you?" he asked.

"I'm one of the airlines nurses, young man," she said smiling.

Danny suddenly sat up. "Where are those men who were with me?" he asked.

The nurse smiled again. "They're not going anywhere just now. We're waiting to hear what you can tell us about them."

Danny flopped back on the pillow. "Man!" he exclaimed. "Will I!"

"Are you sure you feel all right?" The nurse asked.

"Well, I wouldn't mind some breakfast," Danny replied, rubbing his stiff muscles. "Say, would you do something for me?"

"Why not?" the nurse replied. "Right after this anti-tetanus shot. By the way—where did you ever find such an old alarm clock? And the gooseneck lamp, and *bedsprings?* Are you an antique dealer?"

Danny grinned. He looked at his bandaged hand. "I guess I'm a junk dealer," he laughed. "Man! was I afraid I'd rattle!"

The nurse gave him a firm, quick needle jab. "What was it you wanted me to do for you?" she asked.

Danny relaxed his jaw muscles. "I sort of would like to call my family," he said. "I'm Danny Partridge and my sister is fixing our Thanksgiving turkey, and I'd like her to know I'll be there."

"Of course!" the nice nurse exclaimed. "We can't disappoint a sister who's fixing a Thanksgiving dinner! How about some breakfast, and then making your call?"

Danny nodded. He was almost too happy to speak.

Chapter Eighteen

☐ "Keith! Keith! Quick!" Laurie called, clutching the telephone. "It's Danny!"

Keith came sprinting down the stairs, his robe flying out behind him. "Where is he?" he shouted.

Laurie turned back to the telephone. "Danny, where are you?" she asked. "Wait a minute. Here's Keith."

"Danny, where are you?" Keith repeated.

Laurie stood by as the line crackled. "Where is he?" she gasped.

"Shh! I can't hear." Keith wagged his hand at her.

"You're *what?*" he said into the phone. "Having breakfast? *Where?*"

Laurie could hardly wait for Keith to hang up. At least she knew the news was good. "Where is he?" she asked for the third time.

Keith shook his head. "That guy! He's having breakfast, and the police are going to fly him home. I'm supposed to meet a 2:00 o'clock flight at the airport. And if you can believe it, he said he could leave earlier if we insist, but he always enjoys a *lunch flight* on a plane."

"That Danny!" Laurie laughed through tears of relief. "But what happened? Did he tell you?"

Keith laughed. "He told me he had rounded up the gang. He says everybody's under arrest excepting Remi, and Danny's given the police the license number of the kidnap car. That's all. No details—just as if this was only routine for him."

Laurie burst out laughing. "Leave it to Danny." She whirled in a circle. "I'll never get mad at that redhead again! Keith, he's just plain *smart*."

Keith grinned. "I'll bet that you'll be mad at him before the turkey's even roasted!"

Laurie clapped a hand to her forehead. "Thanksgiving Dinner. Oh wow! I'd forgotten all about it! Keith, let's call Miss Penland right away. We'll tell her the good news and ask them to have Thanksgiving Dinner with us. Don't you think we should have a joint celebration?"

It wasn't until Laurie was stuffing the turkey that she realized what she'd done when she'd invited the Penland family. She ran into the living room.

"Keith! You'll have to go over to Barry's, quick. Do you realize what's happening? There will be six Partridges, one Crandall, and three Penlands for dinner. Keith, that makes *ten* of us."

"What does that have to do with going over to Barry's?" Keith asked.

"Tell him to look in their freezer. We need pies! Cranberry sauce! And another turkey—if it isn't frozen hard as a rock! Keith, go! We're going to run out of food, and on Thanksgiving!"

Keith grinned. "Okay, but it's entirely possible Danny will bring along a beautifully roasted turkey himself. He seems to be on top of all problems so far."

"I doubt it," Laurie said shortly. "Please *move*, Keith. You just don't understand the responsibilities of a *hostess*."

Laurie could hardly believe she'd done it! At seven o'clock the family and guests were seated around the

Partridge dining table, and the turkey, golden and beautiful, was placed before Keith. He flourished the carving knife. "Well, here goes!" he grinned. "Give me a G-chord folks!"

They did—even Miss Penland. Pam, radiant in a white wool dress, smiled across at Keith, and he almost forgot to begin the carving. He had never seen her look so happy—and for once, unafraid.

Laurie, flushed from her work in the kitchen, suddenly remembered she was still wearing an apron and turned even pinker. "Just when I wanted *everything* to be perfect—including me," she said to herself. "Barry's probably staring at me and thinking, 'what a dope!'"

But Barry was staring at the magnificent turkey. He shook his head. "Laurie," he said in an awestruck voice, "You mean you did *that?* Man! What a bird!"

And Laurie's face grew as radiant as Pam's. It *was* a day to celebrate—a special kind of Thanksgiving for every person at the table!

Shirley, still bewildered by all of the things that had happened since she had left on Monday, sat next to the bandage-handed Danny.

Miss Penland, dressed in dark red velvet and wearing a shimmering diamond necklace, sat between Barry and Robert.

Even before dinner, welcome news had arrived. Not only were the two men under arrest, but Remi was under lock and key. In the hospital across town, the real Mrs. Gruff was showing every sign of a speedy recovery, and extradition papers had been issued for the fake Mrs. Gruff.

Shirley looked from glowing face to glowing face. Pride in her children welled up in her heart. Danny— whose razor-sharp brain had saved Miss Penland and himself. Keith, whose quick thinking had saved poor

157

Mrs. Gruff and who'd kept his head on his shoulders. Laurie, pink and glowing, being a wonderful hostess at a wonderful meal. And Chris and Tracy—her dear and youngest children!

Shirley almost had to shake herself to hear the words Miss Penland said.

"This is a delicious mince pie, Laurie," Miss Penland smiled.

"It's Barry's mother's," Laurie said honestly. "She's a great cook."

Miss Penland put down her fork. "You know, I've been busily thinking all afternoon. What would we ever have done without the Partridge Family?"

"Been dead, maybe," Robert said cheerfully.

"It's no laughing matter," Miss Penland said sternly. Then she laughed herself. "Well, as I said—I've been thinking."

Danny spoke up. "About the only think I'm thinking about is a wig. How can I make a public appearance in *this!*" He tugged at his inky black locks.

Shirley laughed. "My beauty shop can do wonders, Danny."

"Beauty shop!" Danny gasped. "That's the *final* blow, Mom."

Miss Penland smiled. "Well, as I've said—I've been thinking. Robert here has had a very poor time of it. Pamela has worried far more than any young person should." She hesitated. "And I just think *everybody* should have one great, good time."

There was silence around the table. Then Miss Penland looked at Shirley. "'Of course," she said, "this idea is subject to your approval—but as I reviewed all the incidents that led up to this happy dinner today, one thought struck me. *It's just like a movie.*"

She paused. Nobody said a word. She cleared her throat delicately. "In fact—I can just see Pamela floating around a skating rink with Barry. And Keith playing his guitar. And everybody *singing*." She turned to Shirley. "I've heard your albums, Mrs. Partridge. You have such a fine voice! At any rate, I was thinking—we have all the actors *here*. Robert—for I cannot think of him as 'Rupert'—could write lyrics."

Danny groaned, but Miss Penland went on. "In short," she said, "after your Hollywood concert, would you consider putting this whole episode into a movie? I will supply all the necessary capital. And I think it might be a great success in the name of the Partridge Family."

Danny was the first to react. "You mean it would be *our* picture?" he asked.

"Of course," Miss Penland smiled.

Danny slapped his bandaged hand on the table. "Oh, wow! Oh, *ouch!*" he exclaimed.

"Danny!" Laurie exploded. "*Please!*"

And that was how it all came about. And that was why, on Thanksgiving night, Shirley, Keith, Laurie, Chris, Tracy—and Danny, minus his guitar—were singing heartily,

> "Bump on the head,
> Nobody's dead.
> We're not looking back—
> We're looking ahead."

And wonderfully, happily, grandly—the curtain went down on the most thankful Thanksgiving the Partridge Family had ever had!

Danny grinned. "Hi! Prince!" and he squeezed Robert's arm. "Hollywood! Here we come!"

LOOK FOR THIS TRADEMARK
FOR QUALITY READING